A WHISKER'S BREADTH

A WHISKER'S BREADTH

REG RAWLINS, PRIVATE INVESTIGATOR #9

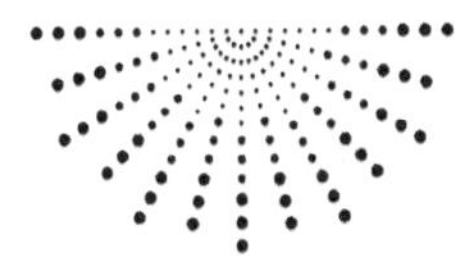

P.D. WORKMAN

 PD WORKMAN

ISBN: 9781989415870 (IS Hardcover)
ISBN: 9781989415863 (IS Paperback)
ISBN: 9781774680247 (IS Large Print)
ISBN: 9781774684955 (KDP Paperback 2 ed)
ISBN: 9781774683149 (Lulu Paperback)
ISBN: 9781989415849 (Kindle)
ISBN: 9781989415856 (ePub)

A Fowl Play on Christmas Day (Christmas crossover story)

Lunar Lies

X Marks the Past

Spellbound Statues

Fur and Fury

Enchanted Mirror Maze

The Hidden Hoard of Drakuntsee (Coming Soon)

Breaking Unboundaries (Coming Soon)

Kenzie Kirsch Medical Thrillers

Unlawful Harvest

Doctored Death

Dosed to Death

Gentle Angel

Rushin' Death

Posed for Death

Death of a Corpse

Endowed with Death

Shattered to Death

Captured in Death

Currying Death

Healed to Death

Death's Charm

Discharged to Death (Coming Soon)

Following Death (Coming Soon)

AND MORE AT PDWORKMAN.COM

For those in need of a little luck.

* * *

CHAPTER ONE

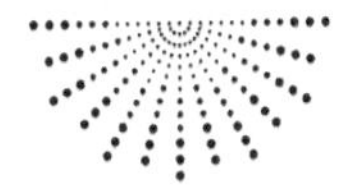

Reg opened the door and got her first glimpse of Vivian King, the woman who had called for a one o'clock appointment. Reg wasn't sure where she had seen Reg advertise, or if she had come by a personal recommendation from another client. Vivian hadn't revealed that on the phone.

She was a black woman a little taller than Reg, her skin a rich, warm brown, with her hair cut short. Reg's own hair, red, was in tiny box braids, just rebraided the day before by Ruan, who might just be her new regular hairdresser, if he stayed in town. But Reg suspected that once his fairy mate had recovered from her injuries, she and pixie Ruan would be on the road again, following a nomadic life since they were excluded from both of their communities.

Pixies and fairies didn't mix.

Ever.

Except for cases like Calliopia and Ruan, which no one discussed.

Reg touched her braids self-consciously, worried that the woman would accuse her of cultural appropriation but, if Vivian had any thoughts on the subject, she kept them to herself. She smiled at Reg and swallowed, looking anxious.

"Regina Rawlins? Hi, I'm Vivian?" Her tone went up at the end of the sentence as if it were a question.

"Call me Reg." She didn't point out that Vivian's pronunciation of her name with long E and I like the Canadian city was wrong, but settled with giving Vivian her nickname instead. "Come on in."

She opened the door wider and ushered Vivian in. Vivian looked around the neat little guest cottage. Furnished by Sarah, the witch who owned the property, renting it to Reg at a price that really was a steal, it was light and pleasant. The scent of the ocean wafted in on the breeze through a couple of windows Reg had left cracked open. Reg motioned to the wicker furniture in the living room, and Vivian selected a chair and sat down, taking one more look around the room as if she were worried someone else might be there watching or ready to jump out and scare her.

People who wanted Reg to read palms usually sat on the couch so that they could reach her easily. Vivian was less sure of herself, putting not only space but also the coffee table between them. She would want something other than palmistry.

Reg gave her a smile that she hoped was reassuring. Nothing to be worried about. It was a safe place.

"Can I get you some tea?" Reg asked, motioning to the kitchen, where the kettle was beginning to whistle right on cue.

"Um, yes, sure," Vivian agreed, which led to some small talk about what kind of tea she wanted. The easy, casual chatter would hopefully help to put her at ease, as would the calming tea and having something to do with her hands.

By the time Reg set the tea service down on the coffee table between them, Vivian was starting to loosen up.

"You have a nice little place here."

"All of the compliments go to my landlord. It came furnished. All I had to do was unpack my bag. Do you know Sarah?" A lot of Reg's referrals came from Sarah, so there was a good chance.

"No. I don't really know anyone here. I'm new in town."

"Oh, okay. Did someone refer you to me, then, or did you see an advertisement?"

"You have a poster up at the grocery store. I just saw it, and thought... why not?"

Reg nodded. She put her posters up on every community board

that she could—even the ones where it tended to get ripped down the first day or two. Someday, the vandals would give up and leave it there.

"Great. Well, I'm glad you called. I'm always happy to take on new clients. You've just moved here recently? Are you planning to stay, or is this just along your way?"

"I don't know." Vivian looked away. "I don't know how long I'll be here. I… move around a lot."

"I know what that's like," Reg said with a smile. She'd been on the move for a lot of years. Her stay at Black Sands had been quite long by her standards. And so far… she hadn't been forced to move on. It was kind of nice to have a more permanent home. Though sometimes it made her anxious and she felt like she should move on before she wore out her welcome. Before anything from her past caught up with her or someone filed a complaint about her. She adjusted the "for entertainment purposes only" sign on the coffee table to make sure that Vivian saw it. The same thing was repeated on all of her signs, business cards, or other promotional items. To prevent any fraud charges by unhappy customers. She couldn't prove that she provided actual psychic services, so it was important to be able to prove to the police that she was providing another legitimate service—entertainment.

"My last permanent place was in Colorado. It's under a boulder."

Reg blinked, sure that she had misheard. "You lived in Boulder, Colorado?"

"No. A smaller town. But a boulder broke off of the mountain and rolled down and landed on my house."

"Oh, dear! How horrible! I gather… you weren't home at the time."

"I was," Vivian nodded slowly. "I was in bed. That corner of my bedroom was the only part of the house that wasn't completely destroyed. They said it was a miracle that I survived."

Reg had heard about things like that happening, but she had never met anyone who had survived such a bizarre accident.

"So… what was that like? You were just sleeping in bed, and then…"

"I heard a rumbling and crashing noises. I thought it was the garbage truck. Then a lot more crashing, and I was going to get out of bed, thinking that someone was vandalizing my fence, or a truck had crashed through a barrier on the freeway. And then there was…" Her eyes were distant as she thought about it. "This huge explosion. Like someone had thrown dynamite into the house. Wood and debris and dust flying everywhere; I couldn't see anything, and covered up my face to protect it. And then some creaking, and… everything got quiet."

"How long did it take for you to figure out what had happened?"

Vivian just looked at her. "There was a big boulder taking up half my bedroom. I could see what had happened, but I didn't really believe it. I just stayed there… in a state of shock, I guess, until the neighbors started calling out and climbing around the boulder into the bedroom."

"Wow. That's amazing. So then they got you out, and you were okay? And you had to make an insurance claim, I guess…"

"I didn't have any insurance. I was just renting."

"You could have had renter's insurance. Then at least you'd get something for the property you lost."

"I can't get insurance."

"Oh." It wasn't any of Reg's business whether Vivian were an illegal immigrant or had some other status that would prevent her from being able to purchase insurance, so she didn't pursue that line of questioning. She took a long sip of her tea. "Well, that's an incredible story. Hopefully, your stay in Black Sands will be much less eventful than that!"

CHAPTER TWO

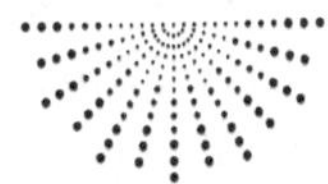

*V*ivian didn't say anything. She just sipped her own tea, her eyes far away.

"So… what can I do for you today?" Reg prodded. "You want me to do a reading for you?"

"Yes, I guess that's what I want."

"You're sure? You don't sound… exactly sure."

Vivian pursed her lips, considering the question. Why else would she have come, other than for Reg to read her fortune or her future? That was what Reg did. She advertised psychic readings.

"Yes," Vivian said eventually. "I guess that's it. I want you to do a reading."

Reg raised her eyebrows, waiting for some other sign of confirmation. Then she shrugged.

"Okay… what kind of reading do you want me to do? I do pretty much everything, reading palms, auras, tea leaves, crystal ball. Whatever you like."

"You can… can you see the future, or just what has already happened? Or tell me that someone wants to give me a message or something?"

"The thing to remember about the future is that it isn't one hundred percent," Reg warned. "I can tell you what I see, but it's often fuzzy, and you can do things to change it. If you make major changes in your life, new decisions that you hadn't considered before, that kind of thing… I don't know what will happen, how it will change things."

Vivian nodded. "I can do things to change it."

"Yes. The future is… fluid. It will generally follow a particular path, with minor variations. But its path can be changed."

As could the past, Reg had found. But she hadn't yet figured out how to explain that even to herself. After years of watching Star Trek and other sci-fi, she would have thought she had a pretty clear understanding of how catastrophic it could be to change the past. But that wasn't how it had turned out at all. The river of time had continued to follow the same course as before, with only minor variations.

But that was beside the point. Vivian wasn't asking about changing the past.

"So how can you see it? I guess that would be a crystal ball thing?" Vivian suggested.

"That would probably be the clearest," Reg agreed. She gave Vivian a moment to think about it and change her mind, then moved over to the shelf to retrieve her crystal ball. "Do you mind cats? I can see more clearly with a bit of help."

"Help?" Vivian looked at her blankly for a minute. "Oh. Okay, sure. Yeah, I don't mind cats."

Reg made kissy noises to call her familiar. "Starlight? Can you come help?"

She heard Starlight jump off of the bed and in a minute, the black and white tuxedo cat appeared in the doorway of the bedroom. He looked at her, blinking his disparate blue and green eyes, then made his way over to join them. He sniffed at Vivian, who politely held out her fingertips to him, then he jumped up onto the couch with Reg. He made himself comfy in her lap, kneading with his claws until she protested.

"Ouch. Enough. We don't need to draw blood for this."

Starlight settled into place. Reg stared into the crystal ball she had placed on the coffee table in front of her. She let her gaze gradually defocus, thinking about Vivian King. She petted Starlight slowly, thinking about Vivian's close encounter with the boulder and the restless wandering that had brought her to Black Sands. She took deep breaths and waited. If she didn't see some stirrings in the crystal ball soon, she was going to have to make something up. She could; she had done so dozens of times before, but she hoped she would see something instead, confirming to herself that she had not lost her gift of vision in the recent trip to the Blue Ridge Mountains.

Starlight extended his claws into Reg's leg again, bringing her focus back to Vivian King rather than the dwarfs and Corvin. Reg needed to remain focused if she were to succeed.

Vivian shifted restlessly, ready for something to happen. Reg breathed out, trying to sort out what to tell Vivian that would resonate with her.

And then she saw it. Something was starting to form in the crystal. Reg stared at it steadily, her vision sharpening.

"I see…" Reg studied it. Nothing special. She might need to exaggerate a little to give Vivian something worth paying for. "A street. A neighborhood in Black Sands, I think. Maybe somewhere you are going to buy a house? Or maybe you've already rented something there… A nice neighborhood… quiet…" Too quiet. Reg needed something bigger to tell Vivian. "Nice houses… gardens… flowers… People with kids… strollers…"

She could see Vivian in her peripheral vision, nodding slightly, but not particularly impressed with Reg's idyllic description. Who would want such an insipid future?

Reg first saw a figure on the sidewalk, and then was seeing the street from the figure's perspective. It had to be Vivian. Her view of the street and the life around it.

"Uh… it seems very peaceful… a good place to rest…"

Vivian shifted, impatient. Then the colorless vision changed. Reg saw something that didn't fit. A big truck, the kind that would take deliveries to a big grocery store, not that would normally drive down quiet residential lanes. Going way too fast, reckless in a street where children might be playing or crossing, or riding wobbly little two-wheeler bikes with training wheels. Reg sat forward, worried, watching the truck. It came barreling toward her, on a downward slope, gathering speed as it went. Vivian was on the sidewalk, so she didn't have anything to worry about, and there were, luckily, no children playing in the way.

But the truck wasn't following the curve of the road. It kept coming down the hill, straight down, straight toward Vivian.

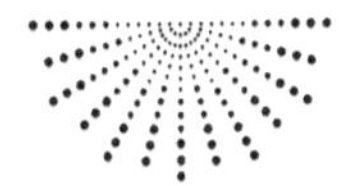

CHAPTER THREE

Reg reared back, putting her hands up as if that could stop the truck in the vision. She couldn't stop something that was in the future, or anything she saw in her crystal. She didn't have any dominion over it; she was merely an observer. But her body reacted as it would have if she were really there, trying to protect itself. Trying to stop a huge hunk of metal charging toward her with increasing velocity, trying to step out of the way when she was sitting on the couch. Gasping as it became apparent that she wasn't going to escape. It was going to jump over the curb and flatten her, and it was impossible for her to get out of its way fast enough.

Reg swallowed a scream and tried to get control of her breathing and moderate her expression before looking back at Vivian. She gulped for air. It would be obvious to Vivian that Reg had seen something terrifying. She couldn't cover that up with a few platitudes.

Vivian's eyes were wide. She was clearly surprised by Reg's reaction. "What… what did you see?"

Reg couldn't deny having seen something. And she couldn't say that it hadn't been anything or hadn't meant anything. She took a few more breaths, trying to slow the pounding of her heart. Starlight stood and rubbed against her, trying to soothe her. She rubbed the white star in the short fur of his forehead, trying to tap into his calm.

"It was a truck," she said, her voice much calmer than she had thought it would be. "I don't know what it was doing on that street; it didn't look like it belonged there. And it was going too fast, not paying attention. Maybe the driver had a heart attack or lost control… it wasn't…. It was going to crash."

"A truck is going to crash? That's my future?"

Reg raised her hands in a helpless gesture. "Um… that's what I saw. I'm sure that's not the only thing that is going to happen…"

"Well, it could be," Vivian suggested wryly.

"No… if you see it, you should be able to just get out of the way…"

"What if I don't? What if I'm not fast enough? Then I'm going to be as flat as a pancake."

Reg chewed the inside of her lip. She didn't like to give clients bad news. She certainly didn't want to tell Vivian that she was going to get run over by a truck and that would be the end of her. But that was all that Reg had seen. She was hesitant to make anything up that might steer Vivian toward the wrong choices.

"I'm sure you'll be able to avoid it. We could set up a follow-up appointment, and I could look to see what else I can see for you…"

"You mean I should come back after I avoid getting smushed by a truck?"

"Well… yes."

Vivian got slowly to her feet. "Okay. This has been an… interesting experience." She dropped a few bills on Reg's coffee table to pay for the session. "I don't know… if I'll be back."

"I'm sorry. I wish I had a better answer for you."

"No one can accuse you of giving plain vanilla readings, anyway."

"Not everyone gets anything quite so… dramatic."

Vivian zipped up her purse and stepped toward the door. "Thank you anyway…"

"Do you want to get together for dinner or something?" Reg asked.

Vivian stopped, her brows drawing down. "What?"

"You sounded like you didn't know anyone in town, so I

wondered if you wanted to do something later. Go out to dinner, have a drink, whatever you'd be comfortable with. I don't know."

Vivian nodded slowly. "You're very kind to offer. We'll see."

Reg nodded jerkily and watched her leave. She reviewed her invitation, shaking her head. "Smooth, Reg. Very smooth. She probably thinks I was coming on to her."

She had been nervous about extending an invitation, particularly since the last newcomer to Black Sands that she'd socialized with had ended up being… something other than what she had appeared. It was going to be a long time before Reg was going to get over Jacky Lane.

* * *

Reg tidied away the tea service and tucked Vivian's payment into one of the pockets of her skirt, and then headed over to the big house to see Sarah. The rent was due and, although she knew that Sarah wouldn't harass her about it if she were a few days late in paying, she liked to get it out of the way right away. For once, she wasn't on the brink of poverty, but the lessons she had learned while she was—like always making sure her shelter was paid for first—stuck with her.

She knocked on the back door and then opened it. Sarah always just knocked and walked into the guest cottage and encouraged Reg to do the same. What was the point in always having to open the door for each other?

Sarah bustled into the kitchen a few minutes later. "Oh, I thought I heard you, Reg. How is your day going?"

"Good." Reg pulled out her money and counted what she needed for rent. "Are you sure you don't want to raise my rent, now that I have the means?" she asked. "I know that to begin with, you wanted to make it reasonable for me, so it's way below market. You should raise it now that I can afford to pay more."

"Oh, no." Sarah waved away this silly idea. "You're doing me a favor by living there. I wouldn't be comfortable with it being empty. Properties are always much safer if they are occupied."

"But you could have someone else in there. Someone else who could pay more."

"No. You're the one I want there, and I won't hear anything more about it. Do you want to sit down for a cup?"

"I just had tea with a client, so none for me. I want to be able to shop later without having to search for a restroom every time I walk into a store."

"Some cookies?" Sarah offered, motioning to a tin on the table.

Reg considered, then sat down and opened the cookie tin. She had a terrible sweet tooth, and she really needed to watch what she ate, or the new clothes she bought wouldn't fit her for long. It was nice not to be starving all the time, but she also didn't want to have to worry about diabetes or coronary heart disease.

"Just one. And I probably shouldn't."

"Oh, one cookie never hurt anyone."

Reg smiled. She bit into the soft chocolate chip cookie and let the chocolate chunks melt in her mouth. "You are such a good baker, Sarah. These are amazing."

"I didn't make them," Sarah laughed. "You know I don't spend a lot of time laboring in the kitchen, unless I'm working on a potion. So many other things that I could be doing. Letticia made these."

"Letticia?" Reg stopped chewing. She couldn't imagine the sour old witch cooking up something so sweet. And if she had… were they poisoned? Or enchanted? Surely Letticia wouldn't make cookies just because she was the leader of Sarah's coven. Unless maybe it was Sarah's birthday or the anniversary of her membership in the coven. "Why did Letticia make you cookies?"

She remembered Letticia's little house in the Everglades, off the grid, completely separated from everything. She had a cast-iron, wood-fired stove. It couldn't be easy to regulate the temperature as she would need to do to make the cookies. None of them looked underdone or burned.

Sarah sat down with her freshly-made cup of tea. "No occasion," she said with a shrug. "She just brought them over. Wasn't that a nice thing for her to do?"

Reg looked at the rest of the cookie in her hand. She couldn't very well put it back with the other cookies, or hide the fact that she hadn't eaten the whole thing. She had just said how good they were, so she couldn't say that she didn't like it or that it was too sweet or she had an allergy. She was going to have to finish it.

"You don't need to look like that," Sarah said. "It isn't going to hurt you. Do you think she put a spell on them?"

"She could have. I wouldn't know the difference."

"Maybe it's time for you to start learning."

Reg blinked and frowned at this. "Start learning what?"

"How to tell the difference." Sarah nodded to the remainder of the cookie in Reg's hand. "Use your gifts to examine the cookie. Tell me what you can see or feel."

Reg looked down at it. She felt a little silly trying to do what Sarah had said, but there was no one else to watch and, if it were a prank, Sarah was the only one who would get any amusement out of it. Reg stared at the cookie for a few minutes, looking for an aura. For any emotion or magic bleeding off of it, like she had seen when she examined Calliopia's dagger. After being told that the dagger was evil, she had been able to see the dark magic that was influencing it and protecting it. She didn't see anything like that around the cookie. Nothing dark and, similarly, nothing light—no special halo to tell her that it was good for her.

She closed her eyes and tried to extend all of her other senses into the cookie. She could smell it, still taste the bite she had taken, and feel it in her hand. But beyond that, she could feel the place it held in the universe, the materials it was formed from, its purpose and place in time. It was, as far as Reg could tell, just a cookie. There were no intentions attached to it, other than that it was to be eaten. She broke off a small piece with a chocolate chip in it, and put it slowly into her mouth, letting it melt on her tongue.

"I... don't see anything special. Just... a cookie."

Sarah nodded. "And if there was more to it, you would be able to see that. You have strong gifts, Reg, and if you exercise them, you will get better at being able to spot spells and enchantments."

Reg nodded. "So... it's safe. It's just a cookie."

"It's just a cookie. It might be dangerous if you are diabetic or deathly allergic to chocolate, but since you aren't…"

Reg took another bite, being sure to enjoy it this time. The cookie wasn't a science experiment. It wasn't a potion. Its purpose was to be enjoyed, and she would do that.

"You can help me to see spells on other things? I should probably practice that."

"Certainly." Sarah selected a cookie for herself and took a couple of big bites. She sat there, chewing the mouthful and looking as contented as a cat with cream. After she swallowed, she washed the cookie down with a bit of tea and spoke again. "If you look around you, you will see many things in my home that are wards or have other enchantments on them. It's one of the ways I keep a happy, peaceful home. One doesn't have such a place by accident."

Reg looked around her. She had been in Sarah's kitchen and other rooms of the house many times, but she had never looked at it in that light before. She knew that Sarah had protective wards there, as she did in Reg's guest cottage. But she hadn't realized that she could see them if she wanted to. So much of life in Black Sands was a surprise to her.

She saw a garland of dried flowers over Sarah's back door and reached out to it with her psychic senses. It felt warm and welcoming. Not just something pretty and fragrant placed there to tie the decor of the room together. It was functional, helping to keep the room safe and secure. Much better than a video cam to record the entrance of intruders.

"The dried flowers?"

Sarah nodded her agreement. Reg looked around again. There was more. Sarah had said that she had many wards and spells.

She could see a sort of a glow over the oven. She had thought it was just the reflection of the overhead light in the chrome but, as she closed her eyes, she could still see it with her other senses.

"I guess… the stove. Is that… to make it so that you can prepare potions that work…?"

Sarah chuckled. "The hearth is a strong symbol of home, safety, and security. In ancient times, it was the fireplace, which is where families cooked, warmed their homes, and brewed their potions. Now… it's the stove. Though it may also a fireplace or furnace if you have them."

"The hearth," Reg repeated. It was a word that brought feelings of warmth and safety. She had heard the expression 'home and hearth' before, but hadn't known what it meant.

Reg finished eating her cookie, looking around Sarah's kitchen thoughtfully. There were many items that seemed to have a bit of a glow. She had thought that they were just well-polished, but there was more to it than that. Magic. Spells and wards. She would be able to recognize them better elsewhere. When she went back to the cottage, she could look for them there too.

CHAPTER FOUR

$\mathcal{R}$eg had stayed for longer than she had intended to at Sarah's house and, as a result, was running late for her meeting with Francesca. It seemed like however much she planned ahead, she was almost always late when she had something to do with Francesca.

She'd had lots of teachers, tutors, and therapists lecture her about her propensity for being late. They would have said that she was avoiding meeting with Francesca due to feelings of inadequacy. Maybe jealousy, seeing Francesca as more successful and better looking than Reg. But that wasn't why.

It was true that Francesca was better-looking, with flawless white skin and big blond spiraling curls that would have put Marilyn Monroe to shame. There was no contest. Reg had always had a *striking* or *interesting* face. Dramatic, but never described as beautiful. As far as feeling inadequate in comparison to Francesca... well, that was probably true too. Francesca was so many of the things that Reg herself was not. Organized, well-read, efficient in everything she set about to do. She was Haitian and had come to Black Sands to avoid the Witch Doctor. Maybe there were other bokors she was trying to get away from as well, but she had been avoiding the immortal in particular, and he had ended up establishing himself in

Black Sands as well. Reg didn't think it had anything to do with Francesca being there, that was just a coincidence. He had been there to look for Weston, another immortal, and to build up his own power smuggling magical artifacts.

But the Witch Doctor was history. Mostly. He had sent his life force out into nine draugrs, animated corpses, which Francesca had charmed into their kattakyn forms, performing a binding spell so that the Witch Doctor couldn't re-form. At least, not for another thousand years or so, at which time Reg expected to be long gone. Francesca and Reg were trying to place those nine black cats in magical homes around the world, as far away from each other as possible. Then even when the binding spell wore off, they would be too far away from each other for the Witch Doctor to re-form for many more years. Not until all of the kattakyns could reunite in one place.

Reg didn't think there was any significance to the fact that she was frequently late getting to her appointments with Francesca. In fact, she was late to most appointments, other than those where clients actually came to her house. Even then, sometimes she wasn't quite dressed and ready by the time they got there.

It was disrespectful. She'd been told that by many parents and therapists. If she had respect for other people, she would be sure to get there on time. But it had nothing to do with respect or with being jealous of Francesca. It had everything to do with being ADHD, bouncing from one task to another and getting distracted from the things she needed to do to get ready on time and be where she intended to be. That wasn't her fault. Not an excuse, she'd been told. It just meant she had to work that much harder to get her stuff together and be on time.

Reg rolled her eyes at all of the voices in her head, criticizing her and reminding her what a failure she was. Some of the voices were memories of those many lectures and therapy sessions. But many of them were the voices of spirits that had attached themselves to Reg. They always seemed to have something to say to her on every topic.

Maybe she didn't have ADHD at all, just too many voices telling her what she should do. It wasn't easy to tune them out and stay focused. Davyn was trying to help her with meditation as part of her training as a firecaster. He didn't criticize her like the parents and doctors of the past, but she saw that same frustration in his face when he had to tell her—for the fifth time—to focus. He was as patient as could be expected, but Reg knew it was a struggle. She got impatient with herself too.

"I'm here," Reg announced, when Francesca opened the door. "I'm sorry, I know I'm late, I thought I'd given myself enough time, but when I got in the car I realized that—" Reg cut herself off and dropped her eyes at Francesca's expression. Francesca had heard enough excuses.

Francesca motioned impatiently for Reg to enter. "I am just glad you were able to take time out of your busy schedule to help me with this," she said crisply. It sounded nice in her soft Creole accent, but Reg still felt the censure behind it.

She nodded, eyes still down. "Sorry," she repeated.

Francesca led her to the dining room table, their usual meeting place. Francesca had more biographical profiles of practitioners from all over the world that Reg was supposed to help her to match with the remaining three kattakyns who didn't yet have homes. They were on the home stretch. Reg being able to find a place for the wild Nico —more by accident than on purpose—had been a major accomplishment.

"Here are the new profiles," Francesca offered, pushing a stack toward Reg. "Maybe this will be our last session. If we can find matches for the last three kittens…"

Reg nodded. She squared the stack of papers in front of her. She hadn't yet revealed to Francesca how poor her reading skills were and the fact that she hadn't actually read a single profile. She glanced at them, looked at the pictures, and asked Francesca leading questions while she pretended to peruse them, eventually suggesting which practitioners might be good matches for which kattakyns.

Reg pretended to sort through them, restacking them in a different order to show Francesca that she had prioritized them.

"This one was interesting," Francesca said, tapping the top one with a long, shiny red fingernail. "What do you think?"

Reg gazed at the picture of a wizardy-looking man in a shiny purple robe. "He seems a little flamboyant. Like he wants everyone to know how magical he is."

Francesca nodded. "I am concerned that his bio may be… inflated. It can be so hard to confirm magical references. Especially with witches and warlocks who are off the grid. It can be months before you find out that someone has… led you down the garden path."

Reg nodded. She slid the profile away from her to start a 'no' pile and looked at the next.

* * *

They had been working their way through the pile for what felt like hours. Francesca's black cat, Nicole (pronounced NEE-cole in Francesca's Creole accent), was sunning herself in the window, batting away the three remaining kattakyns when they approached to play with her tail or climb on top of her for attention. She had taken it upon herself to mother the nine kattakyns, but the chore had taken its toll, and she was clearly ready for the remaining kittens to find their new homes so that she could get the rest she needed. She at least didn't have Nico to contend with anymore; he had been the kitten who refused to listen to her, didn't sleep when she tried to put them all down, and was forever climbing the curtains or starting fights with the others. He was faring well with the dwarfs, who were delighted with the privilege of training a warrior cat.

Reg rubbed her eyes. Even though she was only reading the occasional name or headline in the profiles, her eyes were getting sore and itchy and her body wanted to be up and doing things. She'd never been one to sit for long periods of time. School had been torture. She could totally understand how Nico had felt with everyone trying to press him into the mold of a nice, cuddly kitten when it was his nature to be a warrior.

Not that Reg was a warrior. But she wasn't made for sitting.

There was a rumbling in the distance. Thunder? It hadn't looked like it was going to rain. Florida did have some nasty storms. But the sunlight was still streaming in the window where Nicole was sitting.

"What is that?" Francesca murmured, looking up.

Reg started to her feet. She knew what it was, but her body was too slow to get her out of the chair and to the door in time to prevent what she knew was going to happen.

There was a boom like a bomb exploding.

Reg was to the door first, but Francesca was close behind her, gasping Creole profanities under her breath.

Reg stepped out the door and looked around.

She hadn't recognized Francesca's street in the vision. The perspective had been wrong. She hadn't been looking toward Francesca's house and she didn't know the other houses on the block.

The truck she had seen in her vision had hit a huge cypress tree. She wasn't sure whether the truck or the tree had won. The truck was twisted around the trunk, glass and bits of metal scattered around it, still moving with the momentum of the crash. The tree was splintered, broken at the base and leaning over, but not sheared off. Leaves fluttered down on the scene like snow.

But where was Vivian?

Reg looked under the truck, worried about what she was going to see there. The truck and the tree were both so badly damaged—was it possible that Vivian had been between them, and the devastation was so great that there weren't any recognizable parts left? Reg felt sick. She held on to the doorframe for a moment for balance, then pushed herself away from it, toward the scene of the crash.

"Don't forget to shut the door," she reminded Francesca, not wanting the cats to get out.

"Reg?"

Reg walked toward the truck, anxious about what she was going to find when she got there. Other neighbors were coming out of their houses, exclaiming over the sight, hovering in their doorways, pulling out cell phones to take pictures or call 9-1-1, and some of them heading toward the crash as Reg was.

She wasn't a doctor; but then, she was sure there wouldn't be anything to do for either victim when she got there. There was no way anyone could have survived that crash.

Reg couldn't see any sign of a body on the near side of the crash. She circled around the scene, crunching through broken glass and debris, dreading the moment she saw blood or flesh.

People were gathering around the other side of the wreck, voices full of concern, talking to each other and to someone in the middle of the throng. Reg pushed a couple of people aside and saw Vivian.

Not an unrecognizable horror show. There wasn't even a speck of blood. Vivian stood there, apparently untouched, her eyes blank, uncomprehending mirrors of black. Reg touched her arm.

"Vivian. Vivian, are you okay?"

"She's in shock," someone told her.

Reg grasped her and gave her a little tug. "Sit down. Are you okay? You're lucky you managed to get out of the way!" She remembered the paralysis she had felt when she had seen the truck in the vision. Rooted to the spot, watching it barrel toward her, faster and faster as gravity hurried it down the hill.

"She didn't move," a man said, sounding angry. "She just stood there, looking at it. It swerved at the last moment and hit the tree."

Reg looked up into the cab of the truck, knowing she was going to see a body behind the wheel. But there was no one there. It was empty. A runaway truck? How was that possible?

"There's no one in there. Who was driving it?"

People around her echoed the question. It didn't compute. Either someone had been driving it and had managed to swerve around Vivian at the last minute, or no one had been driving it, and it couldn't have avoided her.

Reg managed to get Vivian to sit on the curb. There were sirens in the distance. "What can we do?" Vivian's skin was ice-cold to the touch. Reg looked around for Francesca. "Could you get a blanket?"

Francesca nodded. Her white skin was as pale as a fairy's. Reg suspected that her own was as well. The blood had frozen in her veins at the rumbling sound of the truck accelerating down the hill and the explosion of the crash.

"We should get her farther away from the truck," one of the bystanders remarked. "It's leaking fluids. It could explode."

Reg didn't think it was going to. She couldn't see a fireball of devastation in the future—just a lot of people with a lot of questions.

Francesca returned with a blanket, which she and Reg wrapped around Vivian, who was still stone-faced and unresponsive, her eyes wide and round, as dark as the depths of a bottomless pool. Emergency vehicles started to arrive. Police asking questions, pushing the bystanders back, firefighters evaluating the scene. They managed to pull the driver's side door from the wreck to display the interior, a crumpled space too small for a human to have survived, but there was no blood, no sign anyone had been inside it when it had collided with the cypress.

CHAPTER FIVE

The first responders verified that Vivian was unhurt and that she could go home if she wanted to. Francesca and Reg took her into Francesca's house until they could be sure that she was fully recovered from the shock of what had happened. Francesca brewed some tea and they sat huddled around the table together, contemplating Vivian's near-death experience.

"You were very lucky," Francesca pointed out. "If you had stepped aside, you would have been killed."

The first responders who had examined the scene pointed out a large rock that had apparently caused the unpiloted truck to swerve at the last moment and plow into the tree rather than into Vivian. If she had stepped to one side, trying to avoid the apparent collision course, the truck would still have hit that rock and swerved, sandwiching Vivian between the tree and the truck rather than avoiding her.

"If you had tried to avoid it like I said…" Reg trailed off.

On one hand, she understood why Vivian had not moved. She herself had been paralyzed when faced with the oncoming truck in her vision, unable to do anything more than to raise her hands to protect herself at the last moment. But on the other hand, Vivian had been forewarned by Reg's description of the impending accident. She should have been on the alert and able to get out of the way before the truck made it down the hill.

Reg had warned her.

"These things always happen to me," Vivian said woodenly. Her first words since Reg had arrived at the accident scene.

Reg could understand. Vivian had miraculously escaped death when a boulder had crushed her house. And now she had narrowly missed being flattened by a runaway truck. The two accidents together seemed portentous. But they were only two unconnected accidents. Lightning did sometimes strike the same place twice. It didn't mean anything.

She patted Vivian's shoulder. "Everything is going to be okay," she soothed. "I know it seems crazy, and like it must be connected to what happened in Colorado. But it's just a coincidence. Nothing to be worried about."

Vivian looked at her with wide eyes. "Just coincidence?"

"Yes. Just... bad luck. Everything will work out okay. It's going to be fine."

"Bad luck runs in threes," Francesca contributed unhelpfully. "That means one more thing…"

"No, it doesn't." Reg shook her head adamantly. Couldn't Francesca see that she was going to make things worse? She should be helping to reassure Vivian, not make her think that some other dreadful thing was going to happen.

Vivian sipped her tea. A little of the color was returning to her face. She kept turning to look out the window that faced the street, checking out the wreck and the damage to the tree and all of the people who were gathered around discussing it still. There were other experts arriving, called by the police or fire department, people who knew things about accident scenes and how to read what had happened there. Reg wondered if the owner of the truck had realized yet that it was missing. What had happened? Had he forgotten to set the brake and it had just rolled down the hill? It was a big truck— what had it been doing parked at the top of the hill to start with? Where was the driver? Off drinking with buddies? Completely oblivious to the havoc he had caused?

Reg didn't know what to say to Vivian to reassure her and nothing Francesca contributed seemed to be helpful. A couple of the kattakyns galloped past, playing a game of chase. Vivian's eyes followed them, then went to Reg.

"Black cats," she pointed out. "They are unlucky."

"There is no truth to that," Francesca said. "They are no more unlucky than any other kind of cat. It is just a myth. If they were unlucky, then wouldn't I have bad luck, living here with them? I had ten black cats at one point. But no bad luck."

"Maybe they don't cause bad luck to their owners. Maybe they only cause bad luck for other people."

"They are not bad luck," Francesca disagreed, shaking her head. "Ask Regina."

Vivian's eyes turned to Reg. Reg shook her head and spoke in a reassuring voice. "No, they are not bad luck. They're a lot of fun to have around. I have a black cat too. Not completely black, he is a tuxedo cat."

"I saw him," Vivian reminded her. "You don't think that... he had something to do with what you saw? Maybe he influenced it?"

"No, no. I've done lots of readings with him, and none have... ever been quite like yours."

"Lucky me."

"I'm sorry about everything that happened. I really am. But that wasn't because of Starlight, or because of what happened to you in Colorado, or because a black cat crossed your path. It's just... something random that happened."

"I have a lot of bad luck," Vivian said darkly.

Reg was curious and wanted to know more details, but she didn't think it would be helpful to ask Vivian to list all of the bad things that had been happening to her. It would just reinforce to her that more bad things had happened to her than seemed normal for an ordinary person. Maybe a lot of bad things had happened to her, but that didn't mean... what? That only bad things could happen to her? Everybody had to deal with a mixture of bad and good things, and sometimes it just seemed like they had a run of bad luck.

Vivian set her teacup on the saucer on the table. She stared at it for a long time, then turned her eyes to Reg.

"You read tea leaves, don't you? Isn't that what you said?"

CHAPTER SIX

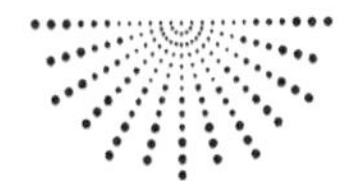

Reg looked at the teacup, anxiety making her stomach tighten and her breathing grow shallower and more erratic. She suddenly felt like she couldn't get enough air.

"Yes," she admitted slowly. "I can read tea leaves. But you've probably had enough fortune-telling to last you for a while. You should… take a break."

"You said after seeing about the truck that I should wait until after it had happened, because then you would be able to see farther into the future."

"Well… yes. But I think you still need some recovery time. Your negative emotions could affect what I am able to see. I don't want to see only negative things because you are feeling… anxious."

"I'm not feeling anxious." Vivian's expression belied her words, but Reg didn't interrupt. "Now that the truck incident has happened, I feel… relieved. I can go on with my life. And you said that nothing else bad was going to happen. So I feel… happy. More buoyant."

Reg picked at her cuticles, not wanting to do the reading for Vivian. Despite Vivian's words, Reg knew that she was not feeling happy and buoyant. It didn't take a psychic to figure that out. And a psychic couldn't possibly miss the dark aura around her.

"You said you would do another reading after the truck accident,"

Vivian repeated. "Was that just because you expected me to be killed so you wouldn't have to do another reading?"

"No. No! I just think… you should wait until you've had a chance for your emotions to settle."

Vivian stared at her, looking her directly in the eye and waiting for her to do it. She nudged the teacup closer to Reg. "Please. I want to know."

Reg looked at Francesca, who shrugged. But what did she know? She wasn't psychic. She didn't have to see the future and stand by her predictions like Reg did. She didn't know what it was like.

Reg grasped the teacup and pulled it toward her.

She looked down into the cup with dread. She wished that Vivian would just listen to her. Or that she had the nerve to tell Vivian no, she wasn't going to do the reading. But Vivian was right. She'd already agreed to do the second reading, and there was no point in running away from it. She might as well do a quick reading of the tea leaves and send Vivian on her way. Then she didn't have to dread it coming up again.

She gazed into the clumps of tea leaves left in the bottom of the cup. Random groupings. She knew that there were books written on what different shapes or symbols might mean, but she had never subscribed to the idea that psychic readings could be taught in a scholarly way. Images in the leaves could only be suggestive. You couldn't read them just one way, like reading the text on a page. Different practitioners could see different things from each other. Reg only knew one way to read tea leaves, and that was by intuition.

Some of the leaves looked like a tree growing up and spreading its canopy across the upper arc of the cup bottom. But they had already seen the tree. The truck had crashed into the tree. Reg blinked her eyes slowly, looking for something else. She saw a house or a cottage. It looked like something out of Little Red Riding Hood, not like one of the houses nearby. But the shapes were symbolic, not representative. Reg closed her eyes. "A tree… a house…"

She opened her eyes again, and let them rest on the bottom of the cup, unfocused, waiting to see what else might come to mind. She thought about cats, cars, Vivian being new in town. Friendships.

Vivian was probably looking for a job. It would be nice to be able to give her a nudge in the right direction. Something helpful instead of seeing something else unlucky. She didn't need a third item to complete the set, as Francesca had suggested. Luck—or bad luck—did not run in threes.

Reading tea leaves was like looking for shapes in the clouds. It had never been hard for Reg's overactive imagination. She saw faces, animals, and shapes in clouds, tea leaves, wood grain, and frosted windows. Her brain was always ready to draw a new picture from the randomly generated shapes.

"A kitchen…?" she said tentatively, trying to make sense of the table and jars of food. "Preserves. Food, maybe this represents bounty. Good things coming into your life. Being able to be comfortably well-off, have your needs met."

Vivian relaxed ever so slightly. "That would be nice."

"Home and hearth," Reg murmured. "The hearth represents safety, peace, warmth, food in the belly…"

"Safety," Vivian repeated in a flat tone. "Do you think so?"

"I know you don't feel very safe right now. Because of what you have gone through lately."

"Do you *see* safety?"

"Tea leaves don't work like that. I have to try to make out representative shapes, and what they might mean. It isn't as clear as seeing a vision in the crystal ball. And even in the crystal, things are often foggy and uncertain. Not as clear as the truck vision." She couldn't help feeling guilty for seeing the truck. Like by seeing it so clearly, she should have somehow been able to tell Vivian how to avoid it altogether. She should have been able to help her, to give her a positive experience.

But Vivian didn't have any control over the truck. She wasn't the one who had set it in motion. It wasn't because of a decision she had made. The only decision she had made was to go for a walk. Why she'd decided it was a good time to go for a walk after Reg had recounted the details of her vision, Reg didn't know. But she obviously couldn't stay in her house twenty-four hours a day. Sooner or later, she had to come out. And when she did…

Reg turned the thought over in her mind.

When Vivian did come out, was there bound to be a truck there waiting for her? As if her destiny were waiting outside her door, just waiting for her, no matter what choices she made?

"What is it?" Vivian asked.

"Nothing. I can't see much more than that… a tree, a house, a kitchen." Reg shook her head. "Does that mean anything to you?"

"That's about as vague as you can get," Vivian snapped. "I'll admit that you were dead on about the truck, but at least that was clear. Now… you're like all of those fake psychics on TV, trying to trigger something by stringing together random images. Of course it doesn't mean anything to me."

Reg shook her head. "I'm sorry. Tea leaves can be vague. I can try another method. Or see if one of the cats will help me."

"I don't think I'm interested," Vivian said. She rubbed her temples. "I'm sorry for being snippy. I'm really not feeling very well. I thought that finally… oh, nothing. Never mind. I think I'd better go home and lie down. Maybe when I'm feeling better, I'll come to see you. Like you said. I'm just not up to it right now."

Reg nodded her agreement. "Probably neither of us is at our best right now. That out there," she jerked her head toward the window, "that was pretty unsettling."

"For you and me both," Vivian agreed dryly.

"Would you like me to walk you home?" Francesca offered as Vivian rose.

"No, you've done more than enough already. I'm fine. I'm only a block away."

Francesca escorted her to the door, standing close as if she might have to catch Vivian if she fainted. But Vivian made it to the door without any assistance.

She nodded at them both. "Thank you for everything. I suppose… I'll see you around."

Reg and Francesca watched her through the window. She managed to get past the accident scene and all of the first responders and rubberneckers without being recognized and stopped. Once she was out of sight, Francesca turned back to Reg.

"I was hoping to finish with the profiles today, but… I think it's been a pretty full day. I'll work with what we've done so far, and hopefully get this done in one more session."

Reg breathed a sigh of relief. She didn't think she could even pretend to read the profiles for another hour. Not with her brain so full of the images of the crash and the puzzling connections between the pictures she saw in the tea leaves. She looked down at the teacup as she took it over to the sink for Francesca. She swirled it once and took satisfaction in seeing all of the images wiped out. She set it in the sink and ran the faucet briefly to further break up the remaining tea leaves and wash them down the drain.

CHAPTER SEVEN

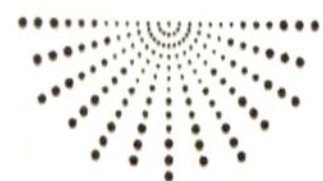

Reg did her best to put Vivian and the accident out of her mind. That wasn't easy. The accident scene had been terrifying, and it was hard to get the images out of her mind. Not so much the things that she had seen, but the ones that she had imagined—thinking that Vivian had been in the path of the truck and had been killed in a horrific collision of unrelenting metal and soft human flesh. There was nothing so terrible about a truck hitting a tree. But thinking about how close Vivian had come to death, not just once, but twice, left Reg a little weak at the knees whenever she considered it.

It was all over the front page of the local paper the next day, of course. It didn't take much to make the front of the Black Sands Post. And Reg didn't actually read the newspaper. But Sarah left a copy out on Reg's counter for her to look at, and Reg nodded gravely and made a few comments about how horrible it had been and how lucky Vivian was to escape without injury, not even a scratch from the flying glass and debris.

They had tracked down the owner of the truck, Sarah told her. "He says that someone must have stolen the truck, because it was nowhere near there, and he was sure that he left the parking brake on. He figures some kids must have stolen it, taken it on a joyride, and then either not have put the brake on, or bailed out once they got it going in the direction they wanted to."

"They think that kids did this?" Reg demanded. "That they started it rolling down the hill on purpose?"

"No one is saying for sure." Sarah dropped her voice to an appropriately confidential level. "Detective Jessup says that it was in gear. It didn't just coast down the hill. Someone put it into drive."

"Was there a key in the ignition?"

"They're still trying to extract all of the parts. She says it was pretty mangled."

Reg closed her eyes and nodded. "It was."

"It must have been dreadful for you, being that close when it happened."

"Especially after seeing it in my vision. And knowing that Vivian was supposed to be there. Or was supposed to get out of the way. I didn't know if she had or if…"

Sarah shuddered. "Well, no need to cry over spilled milk. It didn't happen, thank goodness. Only damage to property, no injuries."

"Yes. No need to keep going over it." Reg picked up the paper and folded it over. "Did you want to keep this…?"

"Oh, no, that's for you. I've already read it through."

Reg put it down with the story folded inside so that she didn't have to look at it again, implying that she was going to read it later. But of course, she wouldn't.

As soon as Sarah was on her way, Reg shoved it into the garbage.

* * *

Reg sat down with her phone, launching YouTube for the latest in entertaining videos. She patted the cushion beside her and Starlight jumped up to cuddle with her.

She didn't have anywhere she needed to be or any appointments in the next few hours and, although she should probably be cleaning the bathroom or vacuuming the living room, Reg just wanted to avoid the real world for a while.

She avoided any videos relating to natural disasters, traffic accidents, or near-misses. There were plenty of cat videos, movie trailers, and entertainment news that she could watch without thinking about Vivian.

At least, not too much.

It was all mind candy to keep her brain from worrying over the truck accident too much, or trying to make out the meaning of the tree, house, and kitchen.

One of the few things she didn't like about smartphones was that her entertainment could be interrupted by phone calls. Even if she chose to ignore them, they still flashed up on the screen until she dealt with them.

She had been ducking Corvin's calls for a while. She shouldn't feel guilty about it, because Corvin was a predatory sort of warlock who could—and had in the past—stolen her powers and was just looking for the opportunity to do so again. But he had also been shunned by the witch and warlock covens in and around Black Sands because of his illegal attempts to take what he wanted from Reg. And she couldn't help feeling bad that he didn't have anyone to talk to. It wasn't really her fault, it was his. But he had also helped her a number of times over the past few months, and she couldn't bring herself to completely ignore him as the rest of the community was doing.

Reg sighed. She answered the call. "Hello."

"Regina." His voice was smooth and silky. Always so enticing to Reg that it sent a shiver down her spine. She tried to pretend to be unaffected. She was getting better at resisting him and, sooner or later, he would realize that there was no point in continuing to pursue her.

"Corvin."

"I understand you've been in the thick of things lately."

"What do you mean?"

"With this King woman, and the nearly fatal accident."

"Yes." Reg spoke through her teeth. "But I really don't want to talk about it. It was… upsetting."

"I can see how it might be."

"But she avoided being killed, wasn't even injured by any of the flying glass and debris. So we all lived happily ever after."

"You know that's a fiction, don't you?"

"What?"

"Happily ever after. There really is no such thing."

Reg rolled her eyes. "It's just a fairy tale ending. I know that."

"Because in real life, every life eventually ends with death. She may have avoided it this time, but you never know when that long shadow is going to come knocking at your door."

"Well, that's a pleasant thought. Is that why you called? To remind me that someday, death is going to come knocking on my door?"

"It's always good to remember," Corvin chuckled. "After all, death comes to all eventually, and if you've avoided certain pleasures and opportunities... then you will eventually come to the point where you no longer have the option, and it will be eternally too late."

"Aren't you philosophical today."

"What I'm saying is, make hay while the sun shines."

"I know what you're saying."

"Maybe I should use a more urban expression. You're not exactly the farm girl type."

"So, you just wanted to call me up to talk about death?"

"No... I wanted to call you up to talk about rescheduling that date."

"We already had a date."

"No. That ended up as a flop. You owe me a real date. One that is just you and me, and dinner and some entertainment. No one else to interfere, no ghostly specters to distract you."

"I can't do that. If I get together with just you, you'll charm me into... doing what I don't want to do."

"I won't." His voice was a deep, rumbling purr. Corvin was remarkably catlike for someone who hated cats. Soft silky fur, but sharp claws and fangs waited beneath. "I will control myself, Regina. You and I can have a pleasant evening together. You will see. Nothing bad will come of it. We can just... enjoy each other's company. No... misunderstandings on either side."

"Misunderstandings. Is that how you're characterizing them now? You weren't trying to ensorcel me. It was just a misunderstanding?"

"You have grown so much in your powers in the time you have been here in Black Sands. Do you really think that I could exercise the same control over you as I did in the beginning when you were just learning about your gifts?"

"And when I was still naive and didn't understand about what kind of a predator you are? What you could do to me?"

"Regina... no more misunderstandings. You and I both know where the other stands now. We have both learned and grown. We're not the same people that we were way back then."

"And yet... you still tried to steal my gifts in the dwarf mountain."

He was silent for a moment. Reg already knew all of the arguments he would marshal against that. She had needed him to siphon off her strength before she blew everything up. She had agreed, in the danger of the moment, to allow him to take it from her to preserve their lives. But she also knew that he had tried to do more than just help her to pull back and stop feeding the fire. He had taken more, whatever he could, and she was still discovering corners of her mind where he had been, where her gifts no longer functioned the way they were supposed to, because of what he had taken. It was disconcerting that just as she was discovering her powers, they had been diminished, and she never knew what to expect from her own mind.

"That isn't going to happen on a date," Corvin pointed out. "You will be fully in control of yourself. You know that you now have the ability to resist me. And more. You are, in fact, more my equal than anyone in Black Sands."

Reg couldn't help flushing in pride at his words. She had come a long way since she had first come to Black Sands, completely ignorant of what she could do.

But was it true? Did she still have the ability to resist him? Or was he so confident because he'd been able to get full control over the powers he had taken from the Witch Doctor? Had he been feeding elsewhere, building up his strength and diversifying his gifts even more? There was no telling how strong he was. Resisting him in the past was no guarantee she'd be able to resist him in the future.

"You know you want to," Corvin tempted.

And she did. Despite knowing that she had to fight him and fear how strong he might be, she was attracted to him. It wasn't just his physical appeal, but also the magical charms he used to reel her in. When he was standing close by and she could feel the heat of his presence and smell the rose-scented pheromones he exuded, she had to exercise all of her strength to resist him. When they were talking on the phone, she still had the upper hand. If she agreed to get together with him—who was she kidding? She knew she was going to get together with him—she would have to be strong and prepared to resist him.

"Where are you, Regina?" he asked softly.

"Mmm. I'm here. Just thinking."

"Thinking about where you would like to go? You chose last time, so it should be my choice this time."

"Did you have somewhere in mind?"

"Somewhere quiet… intimate…"

"No. Somewhere around other people."

"Last time we did that, we ended up with too many people in our party. Neither of us enjoyed it."

It wasn't because there had been other people with them that Reg hadn't enjoyed the evening. It had been the spiders that had bothered her. But she preferred not to bring them up. She still wasn't to the point that she could enter the cottage without first scanning for eight-legged intruders.

"I don't mean it has to be a double date, just… out in the open, not in a private room. Not… isolated."

"Does that mean that you'll agree to it just being you and me? No security guard or police detective along for the ride?"

It probably wasn't a good idea for Reg to go anywhere with Corvin without Damon or Detective Jessup or someone else along to make sure that he didn't manage to charm her. But Corvin was right; she had grown in her powers and was able to block him as long as she was not too tired.

"Maybe."

"You don't need them. You're the only one in Black Sands who is my match. Why would you bring someone weaker along?"

Reg closed her eyes and envisioned Corvin. They had a strong connection and she could usually see him without expending much effort. She had to be careful if she didn't want him to sense her watching him, but she wanted to see what he was doing.

She pictured him at a desk, a big, heavy thing of dark wood that looked like it was two hundred years old and probably weighed three hundred pounds. There were a lot of books and papers stacked around him. She knew he was a historian and sometimes a teacher. What was he studying now?

"What are you doing?" she asked casually.

"What do you mean? I'm trying to arrange a date."

"No, I mean, what are you working on? What were you doing before you called me?"

"Ah." He closed his eyes. "Just doing some research."

"For a class?"

"No. Just for my own interest. There's always so much to learn."

Reg couldn't quite grasp why anyone would study or research something that didn't affect him directly. Not unless he was being paid for it. It was just as unfathomable as reading for entertainment. Watching TV, she could understand. Going for a walk or even a run. That at least produced some feel-good chemicals in the brain. But reading or studying just for the fun of it? That made no sense to her.

Did he have an ulterior motive? Maybe he was on a treasure hunt or was reading up on how to overcome Reg's defenses. "What are you researching?"

"Are you changing the subject? Trying to avoid finalizing the arrangements for our date?" Corvin stretched, rubbed his forehead like he might have a headache and sat up straighter.

"No." Reg knew that he could hear the smile in her voice. A small, satisfied smile lifted the corners of his own mouth in response. "I just wondered."

"Well, I'm doing some research on ancient Egyptian texts, if you really want to know. So much knowledge has been lost over the years—"

"Is it in pictograms? How can you read that?"

"Hieroglyphs. I've spent a lot of years studying the available texts and other scholars' translations. Some of it is right, and in other cases… I think they've missed the mark completely. But not actually having an ancient Egyptian here to tutor me, it's all guesswork, building on hypotheses and assumptions."

"Oh. That must be hard." Reg shook her head. "And this is… just for fun? You're not… trying to find…" She trailed off, unsure what he might be looking for.

"What, the fountain of youth?" Corvin suggested. "The alchemist's stone?"

"Well, I don't know. Maybe."

"I'll admit that lost secrets are always a draw. But mostly… I'm just interested in how they lived. What they believed. What day to day life was like in ancient Egypt and earlier civilizations."

"Don't we already know that? Cave men, and hunter-gatherers, and then farmers. Things didn't really change that much until we started using machines, did they?"

"Those generalizations don't really give us a picture of how the people lived in different parts of the world, though, do they? No flavor of how the people in China lived as opposed to the Native Americans or the Egyptians. Their art, their gods, their writing, and games."

"They played games?"

"They did. Go was played with stones. They ran races. In Peru, they had a basketball-like game that they played to settle disputes instead of warring with neighboring tribes."

"And they had pets," Reg contributed. "The Egyptians worshiped cats."

"Cats were sacred to them. They had several gods who were associated with cats."

"Sound like smart people."

Corvin grunted. "Cats killed mice and vermin. It was a practical thing."

"Cats are very smart," Reg contributed. "I'm sure that was part of it too."

He didn't concede the point. Corvin didn't like cats, and cats didn't like him. At least, Starlight didn't.

"I will pick you up tonight at seven," he said. "You don't want to go to Eagle Arms again?"

The Eagle Arms was a very expensive restaurant Corvin had taken Reg to on their first date. On the one where she had fallen for his charms and ended up losing her powers to him. They'd had a private room and she had fallen for him hard, despite warnings from Sarah and others that she should stay away from him. They were right, of course.

But now she was stronger and knew what to expect. How to protect herself from him if he tried anything again.

She had told him that she didn't want a private room, and she thought that was an important consideration. It was easier for him to work his wiles in an enclosed room, and without other people around to observe. The Eagle Arms had a larger dining room as well, but she didn't want to be confronted with the memories of that date. She didn't want to think about what he had taken from her, and that he fully intended to do it again.

"No. It was great, but… no."

Corvin grimaced. An unguarded moment, not knowing that she was using her powers to spy on him. For an instant, he looked like he regretted what had happened, something he'd never expressed to her.

"Fine," he agreed. "I'll pick somewhere else."

"Are you going to tell me where?"

"I'd rather not have your guards show up there, so… no. We *will* be alone."

CHAPTER EIGHT

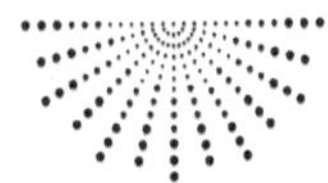

One of the problems with not knowing where they were going to eat was that Reg didn't know what to wear. He had mentioned the Eagle Arms, so Reg assumed that he was thinking of somewhere fancy. Previously, she had borrowed gowns and accessories from Sarah, but she didn't want to have to face Sarah's disapproval over her going out with Corvin again. She'd faced a lot of criticism from Sarah and others for continuing to be friendly with Corvin.

But she was stronger than she had been. She was well-rested and in a good space mentally, so she would be able to resist his magical charms.

The extravagant payment Reg had received from Calliopia's parents meant that she could afford to go out and buy something new. She had lots of time until Corvin would pick her up, so she might as well go shopping. Maybe even stop for a manicure or to have her makeup professionally done.

Starlight watched Reg as she prepared to go out. She didn't need to be psychic to sense that he knew she was meeting Corvin and didn't like it.

"I'll be fine," Reg snapped. "He's not going to be able to get away with anything this time."

Starlight gave a low growl.

"I know you don't like him. But nothing is going to happen this time. It will be okay. It's just dinner. I won't bring him home or go anywhere else with him. And he won't dare do anything in front of everyone."

She pushed away any nagging doubts. Bystanders wouldn't know what he was doing unless they were practitioners themselves. And even then, how would they know whether she had agreed to give him her gifts or not?

But he wasn't going to be able to, so there was no point in worrying about it.

* * *

She walked past Marian's storefront on the way to the dress shop. Marian was one of the other psychics in Black Sands. Reg's direct competition. And she didn't like Reg. They'd butted heads more than once in the past. But Reg had gone to her recently for help, and maybe now they would have a slightly different relationship. Reg glanced inside as she went past the window, and saw Marian's face turn toward her as she walked by. She didn't pause or make eye contact. She didn't want to talk to Marian this time.

The dress shop was just a couple doors farther down the street. Reg breathed a sigh of relief as she pushed the door open and entered. Marian hadn't followed her to the street to talk to her. They had just shared one brief glance as Reg passed by. Not long enough for Marian to read anything.

The dress shop lighting was just right. Bright enough to see the dresses to their best effect, but not the harsh blue fluorescent lighting that many stores had. There was soft classical music playing and a light floral scent hung in the air.

"Welcome," greeted a tall woman with short gray curls and a straight, stiff posture. "I hope we can help you find what you are looking for today."

Reg shifted the heavy purse on her shoulder, feeling awkward and out of place. She wasn't used to ritzy stores. Before coming to Black Sands, if she had wandered into such a place, she would have been kicked right back out again. And she hadn't thought to make herself presentable before entering the store. Her clothes wouldn't exactly fill the woman with confidence that Reg would be able to pay for anything in the store. But the woman was gracious, acting like she knew Reg and her financial situation.

"Thanks. I—um..." Reg looked around the shop. "This is really nice. I'll just look around for a minute..."

"Certainly. Take all the time you need. I'm here to help. We have many options that are not on display. This is just a representative sample. I'm sure we can find just the right item for you."

"Okay."

The woman faded back, stationing herself behind a counter and working on advertising or inventory or whatever was up on her computer screen. Reg wandered around, not sure where to start or what she needed. It would be good for her to get something simple and classic, something that she could reuse at other events with other accessories to get her money's worth. A little black dress or other staple that could be the backdrop to various wraps, scarves, or jewelry.

She made a slow circuit around the store, eventually finding herself in front of the owner's desk.

"So, how can we help you today?"

The woman's name tag said 'Bee,' and for an instant Reg pictured her as a fuzzy yellow and black bumblebee, flying from one brightly-colored dress to another. She flushed at the ridiculous image and looked away, pretending she was looking at a pink dress on a mannequin nearby.

"This one?" Bee asked, moving toward the pink dress. She told Reg the brand or artist name, what sort of events the dress should be worn to, and the various colors and options Reg had if she were inter-ested. Reg nodded automatically, but wasn't particularly interested in that dress.

"I'm going out to dinner. I don't know where we are going, but the guy—the man—I think he's picking somewhere fancy, and I don't really have anything appropriate if it's formal. But if he picks some-place... like a family restaurant... I don't want to look like an idiot."

"Something classic and understated," Bee suggested. "Good for all different occasions."

"Yeah, exactly. And then I can wear it other places too. Get my money's worth."

Her face got hot. She probably shouldn't have mentioned money at such a high-end place. She'd sound like a country cousin.

"Of course," Bee agreed. "Dresses are not disposable; they ought to be worn more than just once."

Reg nodded, reassured.

"Let me show you our Cape Collection. Classic shapes and colors can go from the boardroom to the ballroom..." Bee expounded on the benefits of the dresses in the collection while she took Reg over to a corner of the showroom, pointing out several different styles. She picked up a folder and opened it up on the counter for Reg to see, showing her the color swatches and sizing tables.

There were no prices on anything. In Reg's experience, that meant they were very expensive. In her former life, it would be out of her price range. But now that she had come into money, she didn't need to worry about how to con the woman into letting her take a dress out for a 'test drive.'

She liked the classic collection, but her eyes kept being drawn to a colorful dress on a shiny black mannequin closer to the front of the store. Bee stopped talking and followed Reg's eyes.

The dress had a wide, flared skirt of bright blue, a dark bodice with flecks of color, and a lace-up tie in the back. It was not a solid-colored, classic-shaped dress. It was the opposite of modest or demure. It was meant to attract attention.

Bee's eyes twinkled. "Let's go have a look," she invited.

Reg looked at the dress and ran the fabric through her fingers. She looked at the folder showing other colors and styles in the collection. "These are really pretty."

"The peasant style would suit you. Maybe your hair up. Some simple jewels."

"I should probably get something more understated."

"Would that really be you?"

Reg looked down at the clothing she had worn to the dress shop.

Not a t-shirt and jeans or blouse and slacks like most of the women in Black Sands would have worn. A multicolored skirt, ankle boots, and a scoop-neck, puffy-sleeved crinkled blouse. Understated really wasn't her style. When she had started the psychic gig, she had been delighted to try out more and more colorful and eye-catching skirts, scarves, and headgear. She loved her red box braids and the rainbow of color in her closet. There wasn't a little black dress in the place. She'd never worn such a thing.

"Well, no, I guess not," she admitted. "But won't something like this… stand out?"

"Yes. But not everyone wants to blend in."

Reg looked at the dress on the mannequin again. "Yeah. You're right."

CHAPTER NINE

Reg left the dress shop with a bag full of goodies and nearly ran into Letticia on the sidewalk outside.

"Oh, I'm sorry."

Letticia looked her over. A stern, sour-looking old witch, she always made Reg feel small and inadequate. But she had spoken gently to Reg when Sarah's health had been failing, had served her tea, and spoken up in her defense when she had gone to Corvin's tribunal to testify. And she made tasty chocolate chip cookies. The woman wasn't all bad. There was something soft and warm under the tough exterior.

"You've been shopping," Letticia observed.

Reg felt unaccountably guilty. She clutched the bag closer, as if she had to protect it. What was Letticia going to do? Take it away? Tell her she couldn't afford it and force her to take it back? Reg had paid for it, and it wasn't any of Letticia's business.

"Yes. I… needed a new dress."

"Indeed."

Reg resisted the urge to insist that she really *did* need it. Letticia seemed like every stern schoolteacher Reg had ever had, always catching her out doing something wrong, even if Reg had no idea she had been doing anything bad in the first place.

"I had one of your cookies the other day. The ones you gave to Sarah. They're really good."

Letticia's face softened a little. "I'm glad you enjoyed them. Don't eat too many of them if you want to fit into that dress."

Reg rolled her eyes. "You're right about that. It at least has a lace-up bodice, so there is some leeway. But too many and my investment is going to go down the drain."

Letticia nodded. "You're… going out tonight, are you?"

Reg hadn't said so, and wondered whether Letticia had psychic skills herself, or whether she was guessing.

"Yes, actually. Tonight." Reg didn't know what else to say. If Letticia were fishing for gossip, Reg wasn't about to give it to her.

"I heard you were seeing Damon Knight. Is that who you're going out with?"

Reg shook her head and didn't identify who her date was. Letticia raised one eyebrow, looking disapproving. She didn't say who the next most likely suspect was. She didn't need to.

"I heard you like to play with fire."

Reg was working on her newly-discovered fire casting abilities, so the phrase had a double meaning. She wasn't sure whether Letticia meant it that way, or whether she just wanted to warn Reg away from having anything to do with Corvin. But Letticia's coven was also shunning Corvin, and it would seem she wouldn't even mention him by name. Reg was happy to leave it that way. She didn't have to lie, and she didn't have to tell the truth. She would remain silent on the subject of Corvin, just as Letticia was.

"I don't know where you heard that," she said lightly.

But she could make an educated guess. Letticia had heard it from Davyn, the leader of Corvin's coven. He was Reg's mentor in fire casting and also the equivalent of Corvin's probation officer, keeping track of what he was doing and if he were complying with the rules of the community. The one who would decide when Corvin had paid for his sins. Davyn would have lots of inside information to share with Letticia. Reg would have to be careful what she revealed to him if it were going to get passed on to the witch. Reg had assumed that they had some understanding of privacy between them.

Reg looked pointedly at her phone. "I'd better get moving. Lots to get done this afternoon."

Letticia nodded and stepped aside without a word. Reg navigated around her and Letticia gave her a smile that looked more like a grimace, then went into the dress shop.

Reg let out her breath. She was glad she didn't belong to a coven, or whatever the equivalent was for a psychic. And she was particularly glad that she didn't have to report to Letticia.

* * *

She kept herself busy until the time for her date with Corvin was bearing down on her as quickly as that truck had sped down Francesca's street. She needed the dress, some jewelry, a small handbag so that she didn't have to take her monstrously big shoulder purse, and a manicure. She chickened out and didn't have a beauty shop do her makeup for her. She had done enough new things for one day. She wanted to make sure she still looked like herself on the date, not like some model with all of her freckles blotted out.

The dress fit her and was pretty comfortable. Though it was fancier and much more expensive than her usual daily wear, it wasn't so fancy that she wouldn't be able to wear it to other events or even just for a night out with the girls. Dressed up with a little jewelry, her hair up, and the new manicure, the dress would look elegant. But not so much so that she felt like she had stepped into someone else's body.

Her phone vibrated with a text notification. Corvin.

I'm here. Coming back to collect you. Don't shoot.

Reg grinned. *Come at your own risk.*

In another minute, she could hear his dress shoes clicking on the stones of the pathway. She pulled the shimmery shawl she had purchased around her shoulders and stepped out the door to meet him. It was dusk, the shadows just starting to gather around them so that they could still see each other. Corvin drew close to Reg and looked down at her.

"You look charming, Regina."

She smiled. He was the one who was trying to charm. But she was glad he hadn't gone over the top and said she was breathtaking or gorgeous. She wouldn't have believed that. *Charming* she could believe. Even bewitching.

"You're not so bad yourself."

He wasn't in tux and tails this time, as he had been for the Eagle Arms. But he was spiffed up in a dark suit, white shirt, and tie. He looked buffed and polished and smelled like… himself. A clean, musky smell. Not roses. Just Corvin.

Corvin offered his arm and Reg took it. With several layers of fabric between them, she didn't get the electrical buzz that she felt with skin-to-skin contact with Corvin, but still felt a warm, heart-quickening thrum.

Corvin led her up the path, back to his car parked at the curb in front of the big house. The big black luxury car, not the little white compact he buzzed around town with the rest of the time. He politely opened Reg's door for her, then walked around the car and took his own seat.

The car's engine purred as he turned the key, put it in gear, and pulled out into the street. There was quiet music on the radio. Jazz, she thought. He waited a few moments before saying anything, looking at her sideways to assess her mood and the results of her preening.

"And how is Regina tonight?"

"I'm good." Reg let her breath out slowly, consciously relaxing her muscles, but not her vigilance. She needed to remain focused and ready for any attempt by Corvin to charm her.

It was the first time in recent months that she could say she felt like she was on top of her game; well-rested, strong, and focused. As long as she didn't let herself get distracted with thoughts of Vivian and her accident and the puzzling trinity of images she had seen in the tea. Tree, house, kitchen. Reg shook off the images and nodded.

"I'm feeling pretty good."

"Glad to hear it. And hopefully, you'll be feeling even better by the end of the night."

Reg ignored the innuendo and the honeyed smoothness of his

voice. He really did have the whole seduction package perfected. When he was in pursuit, everything he did was calculated to charm and attract her.

"I guess that depends on where we're going for dinner," she said cavalierly. "Where did you pick?"

"I took the opportunity to get us a reservation at Uncle Mike's, a little off-the-beaten-path restaurant that serves the best barbecue in Florida."

"Off the beaten path?" Reg wasn't sure she liked the sound of that.

"I followed your instructions. It's public. No private dining room. And it's always full."

"You're sure?"

"Would I lie to you?"

Of course he would. Reg gazed out the window at the gathering darkness. "Exactly how far off the beaten path are we talking about?"

"It's out of town."

"Not in Black Sands?"

"No."

"Then where is it?"

"It isn't in any city limits. It's kind of in the middle of nowhere. But you know Florida, even out in the middle of nowhere is still a stone's throw from civilization."

Reg had nearly gotten lost looking for Letticia's house in the Everglades. That was wild enough for her. It would be very easy for someone to get lost out there in the wild and never find her way back to civilization. Or for someone to hide something he didn't want found.

"I don't know about this."

"Trust me. When you taste Uncle Mike's ribs, you are going to forget all about everything else. As far as I know, the cooks don't do any actual magic there, but you would swear it's ambrosia."

The word was familiar to Reg, but she couldn't remember what it meant, other than that something tasted good.

"Ambrosia is…" She was pretty sure it wasn't barbecue.

"Food of the gods. Greek mythology."

"Oh, yeah. Right."

Did she really want him to take her out of town? Away from the relative safety of Black Sands? Though, after everything that had happened since she had arrived there, they might actually be safer outside of Black Sands. Gather a bunch of magical practitioners into one small town like that, and anything could happen.

"You will be safe, Reg," Corvin assured her, putting his hand on her knee. Reg was glad that she had on a long skirt rather than a short one that would have left her knees exposed. She could feel the warmth of his touch, but she could resist that.

"You'd better pay attention to your driving," she advised, pulling her knee away.

"You think I can't drive and talk to you at the same time?" He smirked and rested his arm along the back of the seat, behind her head. Reg shifted, keeping an eye on him.

"This barbecue place had better be really good."

"Oh, it is."

CHAPTER TEN

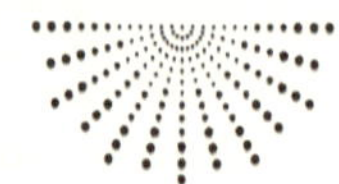

Reg hadn't even thought about how challenging it might be to eat barbecue in their fancy clothes. She was glad that she hadn't dressed any more formally. She felt like she fit in pretty well at Uncle Mike's, but Corvin, even though he had been there before, seemed overdressed. Patrons' clothing ranged from t-shirts and blue jeans, sometimes with bare feet shoved into dusty sandals, to smart button-up shirts, pantsuits, or skirts. But she didn't see anyone else in a formal suit like Corvin's. Did that mean that he had hoped to get a reservation somewhere else, but had been forced to settle for Uncle Mike's? Or did he have something planned for later in the evening that would require more formal dress?

Or did he just like to attract attention and show off how handsome he was? The carefully-trimmed beard and wavy hair moussed to perfection and deep dark eyes would have attracted the attention of nearly every woman in the place without the extra flamboyance of his tailored dark suit.

When they sat down, Reg saw that they had been supplied with bibs as well as menus. She glanced around at the other restaurant-goers and saw that just about all of them were wearing their bibs to protect their clothing, and some of them were very well-decorated with barbecue sauce.

Corvin looked around, smiling. "It's that good," he confirmed.

Reg shook her head. After all of the build-up, the barbecue had better be the best she'd ever tasted. And she'd lived for a time in Kansas City, the self-proclaimed barbecue Capital of the World.

She opened her menu and looked over the pictures.

"Shall I order us a bottle of wine?" Corvin suggested.

"Wine? I thought barbecue went with beer."

He raised his brows. "Well, beer it is, then. Is there a particular variety that should be paired with barbecue?"

Reg rolled her eyes and shook her head. "I don't think it matters."

Corvin perused the 'wine and spirits' folder on the table seriously for a few minutes before waving to their waiter and placing their drink orders. The waiter, a chirpy guy that made Reg think of Jiminy Cricket took the order and disappeared into the kitchen.

"So what's the specialty?" Reg asked, looking up from the pictures on her menu. "Is it the ribs? Or should I get chicken or jumbo shrimp."

"Definitely the ribs. It would be sacrilege to order anything else. Of course, you're welcome to order whatever you like, but we could go for a variety platter and share it…"

She'd objected to him ordering for her before, and she was glad to see that he remembered the lesson.

"Sure, that sounds good. It's not too spicy, is it? I like some spice, but not the kind that makes you cry."

Corvin chuckled. "No. It won't make you cry. Unless they're tears of joy."

More eye-rolling. Reg closed her menu and set it to the side on the table. Corvin looked through his for another minute or two, even though she had agreed with his suggestion. Then he set his menu on top of hers. "This is nice."

Reg looked around. "It is. I like the ambiance. It's friendly."

"I meant it's nice to be here, alone with you."

He was right about it being full. It was a good thing he had called ahead to reserve a table. There were a lot of people milling about the front entrance and outside, having a drink or two while they waited for a table to open up. But Corvin and Reg had been ushered directly in.

She turned back to Corvin and found him watching her intently. She felt herself flush under his gaze. Corvin smiled and looked away when Jiminy Cricket returned with their drinks. The beers were tall and frothy. Corvin picked his up and had a taste. He nodded to the waiter and placed their order for the variety platter.

"How have you been lately?" he asked Reg when the waiter was gone once more. "Any interesting cases? And you are, I assume, fully recovered from your last one?"

Reg had only been in hospital for a couple of days, but it was an experience that she hoped never to have to repeat.

"Yes, I'm good. Everything is working. I'm supposed to do some follow-up appointments to monitor my kidneys, but… I don't know if I'll bother. I feel fine."

"Not something you want to neglect."

"But I'm fine, really. They just want more money for follow-up appointments. They keep you on the string for as long as they can."

"You only have one life. Or at least, only one life here as a mortal human being. I can't speak to reincarnation or the afterlife."

Or immortality. Reg wondered what traits she had inherited from her mother, a part siren, and what she might have inherited from Weston. Francesca referred to Weston and his kind as immortals, but were they really? Or were they just long-lived? Did their children inherit long life?

And for that matter, how long did sirens live? When they weren't killing each other off, of course. Reg had never thought much about the short lifespan of a human being before, but repeated barbs from the fairies and pixies about the shortness of the human lifespan and her recent stay at the hospital had gotten her thinking about it.

That and Vivian's close encounter with death.

"*You've* lived a long time," she said to Corvin.

He gave a slight smile and nodded. She wasn't sure how old he really was. He didn't look over forty, but she had been assured that he was much older than that, kept young by his practice of the magic arts.

"How long do you think you'll live?"

"That's hard to say. It won't compare to the lifespan of a species like the fairies. But… I do intend to stay around for a while, yet."

"Even though you miss people who have already died? Your wife? Grace?"

He looked down. "You remembered. Yes. It's hard to deal with the knowledge that your loved ones will age and die and not be with you for long, comparatively speaking. The transience of human relationships…"

Reg took a swallow of her beer, nodding. She could relate on some levels. She had made and broken a lot of relationships, but she had never stayed in one place long enough for what she could call a long-term relationship. But those people were still alive, out there somewhere on dates with other people, going to their jobs, and living a life without Reg. She hadn't lost them, exactly. Not like Corvin had.

"And do you have children?"

"No, no children." He paused a moment, hesitating. "I would not want to pass my curse on to a child."

Corvin rarely spoke of his nature. She had heard him refer to it as a condition or a hunger, but never a curse.

She had felt his hunger. It had been painful and all-consuming. But when she thought of him, it was usually in terms of how attractive or how predatory he was, not about how he felt about himself and his power. He seemed full and contented when he had fed, so she had always thought of it as being satisfying and fulfilling for him to consume others' powers. She hadn't thought he ever saw it in a negative light.

"Does it always get passed down?"

"No. It's very rare. We know that it is inherited, but not the mathematical chances. I was the only one of my siblings who inherited it."

"So if you did have a child, they wouldn't necessarily have it."

"No. But there's no way for me to predict it or prevent it. And while my kind were hunted down by the pitchfork crowd in ages past, it is no longer considered morally right to kill a child when they first begin to manifest signs of… this hunger."

Reg blinked at him, wide-eyed. "But you wouldn't do that. Kill your own child?"

"Breeders cull offspring that don't manifest true. It's the only way to eliminate negative traits. Whether I could or not… I don't know. It would be a mercy to prevent a child from going through what I have. But I don't know if I could."

"That's horrible."

"Would you want to raise a child like me? As a mother, would you want to live in fear of the day that your child would consume your powers? Can you imagine trying to push him away, to keep yourself from bonding with him, from looking him in the eyes or smelling his sweet baby scent?"

Reg shook her head. "No."

"You would have to in order to protect yourself."

"But *you* wouldn't. Because you would be able to take your powers back again."

"Would you starve your child to feed yourself? Like my father did? Could you listen to him cry for hunger? Or take food from his hands?"

Reg stared down at the table. Other practitioners spoke of Corvin like he was a monster, like he chose to be what he was. But he hadn't chosen that path any more than Reg had chosen to be who she was or to inherit the gifts that she had.

"So, I choose not to have children," Corvin said lightly. "It's best for me and the rest of the world if my kind dies out. And they nearly have."

But he also chose to live a long life. That was something he had control over, as he had said that he intended to continue to extend his life. He could, Reg assumed, end it whenever he chose. Letticia had said that Sarah had lived a long and full life and could give up her life-extending emerald when she chose, and ought to do so. But Sarah was full of life and vigor and wasn't ready to leave the mortal world yet.

And Corvin chose to live and continue to prey on others like Reg.

Reg couldn't think of anything else to say. She watched the other restaurant patrons, and occasionally the TV's over the bar and in the corners of the room. Jiminy Cricket brought their platter, and Reg looked over the bounty with wide eyes. There was enough there for half a dozen people. Ribs with all kinds of sauces and rubs and dipping bowls. She unfolded her bib and tied it behind her neck, feeling self-conscious. But pretty much everyone else in the place was wearing the bibs; she would have looked more out of place if she had chosen not to put one on. Everybody would be watching her covertly, just waiting for her to drip barbecue sauce on her new dress.

Corvin also tied on his own bib without comment, his eyes sparkling.

CHAPTER ELEVEN

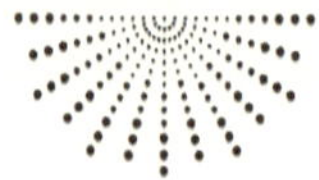

Kansas City had nothing on Uncle Mike's.

Reg had to admit that it was, as Corvin had promised, the best barbecue she had ever eaten. Her stomach was uncomfortably full, and she still wanted to eat more. She had already sneaked into the ladies' room once to loosen the ties on her bodice to give herself room to breathe after the incredible meal.

Corvin had Jiminy Cricket clear the leftovers away so that they wouldn't continue to pick at them and make themselves sick. They relaxed over coffee, waiting for the food to settle, talking more easily than they had at the beginning of the meal.

Even if she could say nothing else positive about Corvin, the man did know how to treat his dates. She had felt the same about the dinner at the Eagle Arms. Reg couldn't imagine a better, more satisfying meal. Maybe his company helped to make it taste better, sharpening her senses or giving off feel-good chemicals like the rose-scented pheromones, something she could taste rather than smell.

She remembered something she had heard about fairies years ago, when she thought they were mythical. "When you eat with the fairies, everything tastes like the best thing you've ever tasted, even if you're really just eating sticks and leaves."

Corvin smiled, and Reg realized she had said it out loud. "Are you asking me if I'm a fairy?"

Reg laughed. "No… just remembering. And… yes, it was absolute perfection."

"I told you so. Ambrosia."

"Right. Ambrosia."

Corvin's expression changed. He was looking at something past her, and Reg turned to see what it was. Someone they knew? A mermaid or siren on the hunt? She couldn't see what had captured his attention.

"What is it?"

"Oh—on the TV. Somebody's not having such a good day."

Reg stopped craning her neck and looked at one of the TVs that was in her line of sight. A "live on scene" banner, with a red crawler along the bottom of the screen, camera lights in people's faces, microphones thrust close to mouths for sound bites. A pulled-back shot of a house where something bad had happened, then zooming in to the tree that had apparently blown over, breaking through the kitchen window and patio doors, causing a gaping hole. There were firefighters and policemen standing around, gesturing at the tree as they discussed how to remove it, cover up the window, or whatever else needed to be done.

Tree.

House.

Kitchen.

CHAPTER TWELVE

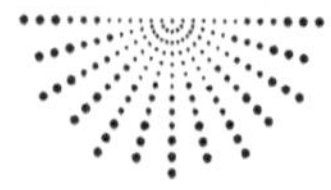

"*O*h, my."

Corvin looked at Reg. He looked concerned. "Reg? You're white as a ghost."

"No ghosts," Reg joked weakly. "Please."

"What is it? You're not sick, are you? You have to be careful not to eat too many too fast..."

"It's Vivian." Reg stared at the TV. Vivian wasn't on the screen. There was nothing in the crawler that addressed whether there had been any injuries in the accident. Or deaths. "I don't understand..."

"You don't understand what? And who is Vivian?"

Reg grasped her beer and brought it up to her mouth with numb fingers, probably holding the glass a little too tightly. She took a couple of large swallows of the beer, even though her stomach was too full already and the alcohol didn't really have anywhere to go except to float on top, triggering heartburn. Reg rubbed her chest, as if that might make it go down.

"Vivian... a new client. She's the one who nearly got hit by that runaway truck."

Corvin raised his brows. "Well, she's having a run of bad luck, isn't she? Nearly run over by a truck and then a tree comes for a visit?

I wouldn't stand too close to her, if I were you. They say these things come in threes."

"This was the third. Her house in Colorado was crushed by a boulder."

"Oh." He blinked. "The woman does have a serious case of bad luck."

"Or she's very lucky," Reg countered. "Any of those things could have killed her and, as far as I know, she's walked away without a scratch every time. They're not saying she was killed or injured by the tree."

Corvin's eyes went back to the TV. "They're not saying her name and they haven't shown her picture, so how do you know it is this Vivian?"

"Because I read her tea leaves. Three images. Tree, house, kitchen."

"Well, that does seem to fit," he agreed. "But we shouldn't jump to conclusions until we know for sure."

Reg pulled her phone out of her handbag. She had been careful not to look at it until that moment. It was too easy to get distracted by a message or pop-up. She didn't want to let the date pass by with her eyes pasted to the phone screen instead of enjoying the time with Corvin. Or to give him the chance to charm her while she was distracted by her screen.

"I hope you don't mind..." She scrolled through her call log, looking for the unfamiliar number. She tried to pinpoint exactly when Vivian had called her for an appointment. "This one..."

She tapped the number and waited for an answer. The phone went right through to voicemail. Probably turned off. That was what Reg figured she would do if she were in the middle of a disaster being reported on TV and didn't want to be bothered by a deluge of callers.

"She's not answering."

"I wouldn't either."

"No," Reg agreed. She sighed and put her phone back away. "I guess I'll try again in the morning."

* * *

The date had been nice, and Corvin hadn't attempted to charm her throughout the evening. Reg knew that he hadn't reformed. He was just waiting for the right time. And now they were getting to it. She was tense as they drove over the lonely roads that led away from Uncle Mike's. She watched him for any sign of a threat, already building a protective psychic barrier around herself. He could pull over anywhere, on any of the little gravel roads, into a thick stand of vegetation that would hide the car from view. No one would be able to see or stop him.

Corvin's hand moved away from the steering wheel, and Reg flinched away. He turned the radio on. "Calm down, Reg. Just relax."

"I am relaxed." It was, of course, a bald-faced lie, and Corvin knew it.

He glanced at her a couple of times as he drove, mouth set in a grimly amused smirk. "We've had a very pleasant evening. Why ruin it now?"

"I'm not ruining it. I'm just being careful."

"You don't need to worry."

But she knew she did. Of course he would tell her that. He would tell her whatever he thought he needed to, promise whatever she wanted him to, and then take his opportunity.

"I'm driving. What do you think I'm going to do while I'm driving?"

He was already doing it. Despite his denial, the interior of the car was uncomfortably warm and beginning to smell of roses. Reg breathed shallowly through her mouth and focused on blocking him.

When he had gotten into a fight with Damon in the coffee shop, Reg had even been able to freeze him in his tracks. She was that strong.

She could protect herself.

CHAPTER THIRTEEN

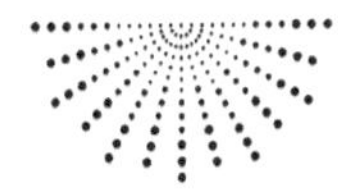

Reg was relieved as they got back into town. Despite telling herself that she was strong enough to withstand him, she was afraid of those lonely country roads. She didn't want to have to face him there, in the middle of nowhere, with no one around to help or know that something was wrong. She didn't want to be left wandering in some isolated area, the voices inside her head gone, trying to get back to civilization before she went mad or passed out in a ditch.

At least in town, she could call for help. If he abandoned her, she could call someone; walk into a store or restaurant or bang on someone's door and be able to talk to another human being. Even if they couldn't understand what had happened to her, they would at least understand that her date had assaulted her.

She unclenched her hands. She hadn't even realized how tightly she'd been trying to hold on to nothing. Reg took a couple of deep breaths, but the floral scent inside the car was heady and made her dizzy. Another breath, and she would be falling for him again. Reg pressed the button for her window. It was locked.

"Unlock the window. I need some air."

"Just adjust the A/C," Corvin advised, gesturing to the vents. "It's cold outside."

"It's not cold. And I want fresh air, not recirculated. Let me open my window or I'm getting out of here."

He raised an eyebrow, amused, and studied her. Reg put her hand on the door handle. She looked down to see where the door lock was so that she could unlock it and open it in one smooth movement. Then she'd have to be ready to jump, even if she was in a skirt. They were still moving at a pretty quick clip.

Corvin looked away and clicked a switch on his armrest. "There. Unlocked."

"Thank you." Reg rolled her window down. She breathed fresh air. Her head cleared a little.

Corvin did not take the exit for Reg's house. Reg gripped her armrest. "Hey. You missed it."

He shook his head. "We're not going home yet. The night is still young. And I happen to know you don't go to bed early, so don't try that one on me."

"And you can't keep me out until I get too tired to defend myself. So take me home."

"Not yet," he said calmly.

"Corvin!"

"We're out for a nice date. Where we go and what we do is my choice tonight. And I say we're not done yet. When you chose the place, you got to choose when we were done."

And Reg had been sick and overcome by a vision. She'd wanted to go home, and she'd sent Corvin away early. He didn't want to go home early this time.

Reg watched out her window, wondering where they were going. She tried to read Corvin's intentions, infringing ever-so-slightly on his mind to find out.

But his walls were up too. He was blocking her just as she was blocking him. What was he afraid of? What was she going to do?

"Exactly what you're doing," Corvin said. "Trying to creep in where you're not welcome. You know it's bad manners to enter someone else's mind without their permission."

Reg glared. "And what are you doing?"

"Protecting myself."

"You're listening to my thoughts!"

"In my defense, you opened yourself up to me by trying to read mine."

Reg grumbled and shook her head. "Why don't you just tell me, then?"

"Why don't you ask?"

"Where are we going? What do you have in mind?"

"I thought we would go to the marina. Watch the boats coming and going. They're quite lovely with their lights on this time of night."

She looked for an argument. If he'd suggested coffee or dessert, she would say she was full. If he suggested going back to her house for a visit, she would tell him he couldn't come in. Watching the boats did sound like a pleasant pastime, but she wasn't sure how things would progress with the two of them so close together with nothing to do.

He couldn't be trusted.

Corvin looked at her briefly, then back at the road. "I told you we would have a nice night."

"I know. But I also know you're still trying to charm me."

"No. It's just a date. Just the two of us enjoying some time together."

"You can't deny that you're trying to charm me."

"Can't I?"

"I can smell the roses. Feel the heat. I know you're trying to magick me."

"You're wrong. I'm trying to keep myself under control. What my body does instinctively, I can't help that. I'm doing my best to rein it in. But you might as well tell yourself not to get sweaty hands when you're nervous. It's not something you can consciously stop."

Reg rubbed her palms on her skirt.

"I've heard this line before," she reminded him. "The whole 'I can't help myself' doesn't fly with me."

"You're so lovely…"

"And if you can't help yourself, you'd better take me back home, because I don't want you to 'slip' and have an accident."

"And you smell… so… enchanting."

"Corvin."

He put his arm on the back of the seat again. The hairs on Reg's neck stood up. She felt her whole body reaching out toward him, longing for him. She fought off the desire to shift closer to him, to take his hand and put it on her neck. To snuggle into him.

"No." Reg concentrated on her shield. She reflected the heat back to him, which she'd had success with in the past. Corvin loosened his tie, uncomfortable. He reached over and turned up the air conditioning.

"Would you close your window, please? The air conditioner does not work well with it open, and it's getting… a little uncomfortable here."

"Then maybe you should pull back on the heat. Maybe have a cold shower."

"I'm not going home. We're going to the marina."

"I'm sure we could find a hose there."

Reg thought that the air around her got a bit cooler. She shifted her position, trying to stretch out muscles that she'd been holding tense. Her whole body felt like one giant knot.

"How much farther?"

"Five minutes, if that."

"Can we get out of the car?"

He didn't answer right away. Then he nodded. "Certainly. Of course. Very romantic, sitting on the wall or walking down to the beach. We can take off our shoes. Let down our hair…"

Reg felt her braids, tied up in a knot on top of her head. She wasn't going to start taking the pins out on the beach. She'd lose them and end up with half of her hair up and half down, like some mad woman. "Not literally," she told him. "This took almost an hour to get arranged."

Corvin chuckled. "Fine, then, you can leave your hair up. It's not a requirement."

Reg watched the horizon for the marina. In a couple of minutes, they were winding their way down to it. She could see the lights of the boats out in the water, winking and twinkling in the darkness, reflected up again by the black water.

"It's so pretty!"

"I told you."

Corvin drove around for a bit, looking for a good parking spot, and then settled on one. "It's not as close as I would like. It's going to be a bit of a walk to get down to the water. Are you okay with that?"

Reg took off her heels in the car. She didn't want to wreck them or lose them in the sand.

"We have to walk a bit before we're down to the beach," Corvin warned. "You'll want to keep those on for the first bit."

"No. I'm just going to leave them in the car."

He shrugged and shook his head. She knew, even though she couldn't see them, that he was rolling his eyes at her stubbornness.

They each opened their doors. Reg put her bare feet down on the pavement. It still held a little of the heat of the day. She only took a step or two before she knew that Corvin was right. Gravel and glass on the pavement made it painful to walk on without shoes. She veered to the side where there were sand and clumps of grass—mixed with gravel and glass—and that was, at least, a little better. She winced as she walked. While she tried to pick out the safest path in the dark, she kept stubbing her toes on rocks, turning her ankle, and scraping and poking her feet with the gravel and debris mixed in with the black sand.

Corvin walked close to her, smiling to himself at what a fool she was. He offered her his arm, but Reg didn't take it. It was hard enough to make her way down to the water without being distracted by the warm buzz she would get as soon as she touched him. He would happily sweep her off her feet, but she might never get grounded again.

"This is nice," Reg said determinedly, trying to keep a casual conversation going to distract both of them from her troubles. Her feet were going to be red and raw by the time they got back to the car. The next time, she would need to take a pair of flip-flops along with her. They would allow her to get down to the water comfortably. And she could easily carry them if she wanted to walk barefoot and found a strip where she could do so without injuring herself. "Do you bring a lot of women here?"

"No." Corvin was standing far too close to her. "Just you."

"Why? What made you choose this?"

"I don't know… I just tried to think of what you would like to do. It was more intuitive than reasoned… you just seemed like… someone who would enjoy the water."

"Are there a lot of people around here who don't like the water?" Reg laughed. "I can't imagine living here if you didn't."

"People can't choose where to be born. And often don't have a lot of choice over where they can find work, or where they get transferred. We have a lot of retirees who come here just because of the water, of course, but… you'd be surprised at how many people there are in Florida who don't like the water or don't know how to swim."

Reg pondered that as they walked. Either the sand was getting softer, or she was growing more accustomed to it.

Reg had always enjoyed swimming. She didn't do well at very many things, but she was actually a very good swimmer. She loved the feeling of the water around her, the sensation of weightlessness, the way her muscles worked together. Even the breathing came naturally, and she didn't need to come up for air very often. Water was her element.

Corvin reached for her hand and, this time, Reg let him take it. She flinched at the initial electrical charge, but held on to him firmly, and it subsided into a background buzz. Corvin's hands were smooth and strong, his grip firm and protective. He was so warm.

Reg took in a deep breath and let it out again. She no longer found it necessary to hold herself tense to be wary of him. She was aware of every little thing that he did, but didn't feel threatened by him. She felt his charms, felt the heat and smelled the scent of roses in the wind that blew past her face, but she was stronger than some roses. She was stronger than anything he could use on her.

She had to remind herself firmly about the Witch Doctor and the amount of magic Corvin had stolen from him and the smuggled artifacts in the warehouse. Corvin had a lot of power, if he chose to use it. And if he had mastered it. Harrison had said that he hadn't mastered his powers yet. That was why it had taken more than just him to overcome Weston.

Reg looked out over the black water. She felt so at home there. She remembered a picture from Sunday School years ago, when she had gone to church with one of her foster families. Moses, in a little basket woven from reeds, floating on the river. She could picture herself floating on top of the sea, rising and falling with the waves rocking her to sleep. She loved the smell of the salt in the air and the rhythmic waves lapping at the beach. There were others there, teenagers laughing and drinking, other couples walking hand in hand, solitary figures coming and going in the darkness. Even though there were other people there, Reg felt like they were alone in their own little bubble. Separated from everything else. She was in her own little pocket of paradise.

Corvin slipped his hand away from hers and put his arm around her waist instead, pulling her closer to him. Reg knew it was a dangerous move, and that she should be alarmed, but she wasn't. She was comfortable there, with his arm around her. She felt perfectly safe. Corvin leaned in toward her. She could feel the heat he exuded and the delicious smell. He kissed her neck lightly and she let him, still alert to every movement, even the beating of his heart, and yet not afraid.

"Come closer to the water," she urged.

Corvin didn't object. They walked closer. Reg felt the pull of the sea. She had always liked living close to the ocean. Even in the north where the water was cold, she always liked to be near the ocean.

They reached the packed wet sand where the tide had gone down. It was easier to walk on. The temperature of the water when it lapped up at their feet from time to time was delicious. Like a bathtub. Her own huge, endless bathtub. She stepped down the beach so that the water was over her feet. Corvin had removed his shoes and socks by then and carefully rolled up the bottom few inches of his suit pants. Reg's long skirt was getting wet and clinging to her legs, but she didn't care.

It felt right.

It all felt just right.

CHAPTER FOURTEEN

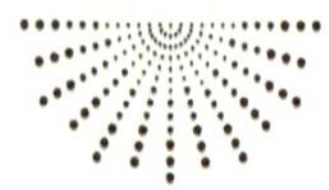

Reg took a few steps into deeper water. Above her ankles. Partway up her calves. Corvin resisted.

"Let's just walk at the edge."

"No." Reg's voice was firm. "I want to be in the water."

"Well, no farther," Corvin negotiated. "I'm not up for a midnight swim."

"You chose the place. Don't I get to choose what we do here?" She took another step deeper.

Corvin pulled away from her, staying where he was. "Regina."

"No." Reg used her index finger to hook Corvin's belt and tried to pull him deeper into the water. "Come with me."

"Reg." Corvin pulled back harder. His eyes were getting big and round. Reg's eyes had adjusted to the dark and she could see every detail. "Reg, no."

She pulled harder, forcing him to take a small step farther into the water, even though he didn't want to.

"Regina."

She wrapped her arms around his neck and went in for a kiss. Corvin was startled for a minute, still trying to pull back, but not wanting to pull away from the embrace or her inviting lips. Reg held herself to him. "Come," she murmured. She pulled him toward her.

Another step or two into the water. She was up to her knees. Corvin pulled back from the kiss. His expression was alarmed.

"No. Reg. Release me. No!"

He had shared his hunger with her once. A deep well of need, a gaping hole that had to be filled. Hunger so deep that it hurt. What Reg was feeling was hunger of a different sort. Not one that would be sated by taking Corvin's powers, but by taking *him*. She wanted him with her, deep in the water, filling all of her needs. She tightened her arms around his neck, even though he was fighting back in earnest. He pushed and twisted and tried to pull away.

"Don't," Reg ordered. "Just come! I'm not going to hurt you."

But even though she told him that, she was aware that she was squeezing his neck more tightly, looking for the warm pulse point. If she squeezed that then, in a few seconds, he would be out like a light, and she could take him with her into the water.

Corvin writhed. Reg used her connection with him to drain his strength. His physical strength was greater than hers, but she knew how to pull it from him for her own use. Just as she had done before when she needed his power.

Corvin swore. He tried to shove her away. He put up psychic blocks, but Reg's psychic gift was her strongest, and she knocked down his barriers as fast as he could put them up. Reg laughed.

"Quit playing games! You brought me here!"

"Regina!" His voice was desperate. "Think about what you are doing! This isn't you. This isn't what you are like. You don't want this."

"Yes. I do."

"You want to be like your mother? You want to give in to Norma Jean's nature?"

The name cut Reg like a knife. She snapped her teeth at him, furious that Corvin would say the siren's name. Norma Jean had no place in Reg's territory. She had no business laying claim to Reg's chosen one.

The physical contact between them was broken. Reg advanced on Corvin, trying to touch him again.

She would force him into the water.

That was where they both belonged.

CHAPTER FIFTEEN

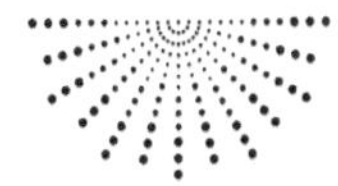

It was like Reg was watching herself. Watching her body do something that she would never have chosen to do. Something else had taken over her brain. An instinct. A hunger. A need.

Corvin avoided her grasp as Reg advanced on him, trying to get him under her control once more. It was almost comical, the smaller woman chasing the strong, powerful warlock. But she had seen Corvin brought under the power of another woman before. Her mother, Norma Jean, when her siren instinct had taken control.

Reg had been disgusted, glad that she hadn't inherited that nature from her biological mother. That would have been too much.

But had it been buried there all the time, just waiting for her to mature enough and to go back to the ocean, where she could overcome her prey and take him under the water?

Corvin was several yards away from her, still watching, careful that she couldn't launch herself at him and get him under her control again.

"Reg!"

"I don't want to do this!" Reg resisted the pull as much as she could. But the water tugging around her legs fed the hunger and need. "Stay away from the water," she told Corvin. "I think it's something in the water."

"I don't think it's going to affect me," Corvin said in a voice that attempted to be calm and reassuring. "It's just you. Maybe you should come out of the water."

"No. No, I need to…" Reg looked up and down the beach, following the water in each direction. Maybe there was someone else. Someone who was close to the water's edge who would go in with her without asking the reason. Who needed a reason? She was just following her heart.

"Reg, just come toward me. Out of the water. Come this way…"

He beckoned to her, inviting her to come out. His movement wafted his scent closer to her, driving her mad.

"Corvin!"

He took another step away. Reg needed him to step closer, not farther away. She needed to stop him.

She dashed at him, hoping to catch him off guard. She could knock him off balance, maybe even hit him in the head, and then in his confused state, he would be easy to pull back to the water.

But her run toward him took her out of the water, past the packed wet sand, into the loose, dry sand that was harder to walk or run through. Corvin took a couple of steps back, leading her on through the dry sand mixed with gravel that cut her feet.

"Let's go home, Reg. It's getting cold. You're getting tired."

She was angry with him for walking away. It wasn't fair. It wasn't right. She'd had him in the water. She'd been *that* close.

"Where are you going?"

"Back to the car. We can sit and talk there."

"No! No, I don't want…" She couldn't think of what it was she wanted. Her brain was muddled.

"Come on." He continued to walk back toward the car. Reg, stumbling and clumsy, tried to match his pace or to catch up so she could take him back to the water.

She was mincing by the time they got back to the car, her feet in exquisite pain. She wanted to go back to the soothing water and smooth, wet sand.

Corvin used his key fob to unlock the car. Its lights flashed. Corvin got in on his side. He didn't hold Reg's door for her.

Reg opened the passenger door and slid into her seat, angry and frustrated.

* * *

For a few moments, they just sat there, both breathing heavily, pondering what had happened.

"Well. That was unexpected," Corvin said dryly.

Reg breathed out. "What just happened?"

"I think you know the answer to that."

"No. I don't get it. Nothing like that has ever happened before. It doesn't make any sense."

"If Norma Jean was part siren, then it makes perfect sense. You're her daughter."

Reg shook her head adamantly. "No. There's something in the water here. Or a spell. It enchanted me."

Corvin was watching her carefully. "I won't say that's impossible, but I think it's unlikely. No one else was affected. Only you."

"But if I had any kind of… siren instincts…" Reg rolled her eyes at the idea. "Then they would have shown up before now. Why would I not be affected by them until now?"

"Maybe it was just the right combination of circumstances. After dark, walking on the beach, a… suitable target at hand."

"I've been swimming lots of times. I've never had anything happen. It wouldn't be the first time I took a late-night dip in the ocean. Though, up north, the water was never as warm as it is here."

"By yourself, or with someone else?"

Reg thought about it. "I've been swimming with boys."

Corvin shrugged. He scratched his beard. "Maybe there is something special about the water here. Or you weren't old enough for it to have kicked in yet."

Reg stared through the windshield at the boats, festooned with lights, moving into and out of the marina.

"Or it could be that meeting your mother triggered something. A genetic memory or on-switch."

"You were kind of *out of it* at the time. But she told me that this would be my territory. To stay away from her waters."

"Competition can trigger different behavioral patterns. Some species even change sexes if the opposite sex is in short supply."

"Well, I hope *that* isn't going to happen."

Corvin allowed a small smile. "I haven't heard of that happening with humans or sirens."

"But who knows what else might be in the mix."

Corvin opened his mouth, then closed it. Reg rubbed her forehead. It was throbbing with pain.

"I'm sorry…" she told Corvin. "If that's worth anything."

"Of course. I know this wasn't something you planned out. I was the one who brought you to the marina. And I do understand something of… instinctual behaviors."

So there they were. Was Reg a natural predator like Corvin? It was something she could never have imagined. She wasn't the kind of person who enjoyed hurting others. She'd always been the one to stand up against bullies, even though they were hurting someone else and she was putting herself in the line of fire. She could just never countenance it.

Even watching herself as Reg had, she couldn't believe that had actually been her. Was she losing her mind? Maybe it was all just a bad dream.

When was she going to wake up and find that everything had gone back to normal?

"I think… maybe I should go to bed." She covered her face, trying to hold herself together.

Corvin put his hand on her shoulder. "Reg… it will be okay."

"It will be okay? I'm falling apart. I'm losing my mind. I can't control my own behavior. That's not okay! That's never going to be okay!"

"I know you're upset. You have every right to be. But this isn't the end. It's just… a bump in the road."

"You could be drowned on the bottom of the ocean! How can you say that?"

"Because… I know how it is to be different. And because I'm not drowned on the bottom of the ocean. You didn't do that. You might have wanted to do that, but you didn't."

"Only because you pulled away."

"No." Corvin shook his head. "You could have incapacitated me, but you didn't."

"I don't know how to do that. Whatever it was Norma Jean did to enchant you."

"Maybe not yet. But you have stopped me before, blocked me using magic, not your physical body. And you could have snapped my neck or choked me out. You chose not to do that."

"How do you know that?" She'd had her arm over his artery. The one that would feed oxygen to his brain. She'd known on an instinctive level that if she'd cut off that blood flow, he would not have been able to fight her any longer.

"I know," Corvin said softly. "And I know that you were telling me to get out of the water. That you said you didn't want to hurt me."

"But then I… I still would have."

"This is the first time that you've had to fight this instinct, and you were able to do it. Next time it will be easier."

"Is that how it is for you? It's easier when you resist?"

He looked away from her. His answer was clear. Reg's heart felt like it was being squeezed. She tried desperately not to let the hot tears escape her eyes.

"Please take me home."

Normally he would have teased her, told her he'd be happy to take her home. He would have made it a joke and an invitation and tried to work his way past her defenses.

But he didn't.

He put his key in the ignition and backed the car out of the parking spot.

CHAPTER SIXTEEN

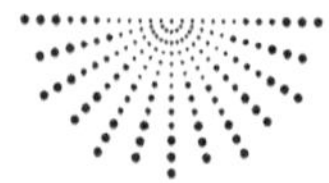

Corvin drove her back to the cottage. There was no teasing, no attempt to charm her. She would normally have been ecstatic that he wasn't trying to use his charms on her, but it threw her off balance.

Was he no longer interested? Was he repulsed by what he had seen her do? Or was he tired after the struggle and didn't have the energy to charm her? She didn't know how to take it.

When they reached the house, he seemed more his normal self. He walked around the car to open the door for her and, when she opened it without waiting for his help, he still took her by the arm to escort her back to the cottage.

"You dare to touch me after that?" Reg demanded.

His fingers slid away from her and he studied her. She could feel his wariness, his uncertainty whether to still consider her a threat. Away from the water, was she back to her normal self? Or, once awakened, would she continue to see him as prey?

Reg wouldn't mind knowing that herself.

"Let me help you, Regina." His tone was smooth and silky, like it always was when he was trying to seduce her. He was good at hiding what he was feeling. Without her psychic powers, she probably wouldn't have been able to tell.

What would happen if he tried to take her powers now? Were her siren instincts something that he *could* take? He'd suggested that he could once before, but Reg wasn't sure it was true. He'd just wanted an opening. What she had felt hadn't been the same as any of the gifts that she had. It wasn't something that she could wield and control. It was something that had controlled her.

"If you tried to take it, would you become a siren?" Reg asked, as they walked slowly down the dimly-lighted path. "There aren't any male sirens, are there?"

"Well, there are, yes. Very rare though, which is why the bloodlines are getting thin."

"So would you become a siren?"

"No." Corvin shook his head, frowning. "I couldn't become another species."

"So you couldn't take… whatever. The part of me that is a siren. Right?"

They stopped at Reg's doorstep. Corvin faced her, holding both of her arms gently, her sleeves protecting her from skin-to-skin contact.

"You will always be part siren. Neither of us can change that. But I may be able to… dampen some of those abilities. The ability to ensorcel a man… maybe whatever strength you get from the water…" He shrugged. "I wouldn't know until I tried."

"But I didn't do that. I didn't ensorcel you like Norma Jean did. So I can't do that anyway."

"Maybe. You weren't really trying, were you? But I've always found you… captivating."

Reg thought about that. He'd often said that he found her more attractive than others he could have pursued. He wanted to consume her gifts even when he'd built up his strength from other sources. She was his 'dessert.' Was that because she gave off some kind of sireny vibes? Or just his ego because she was the one person he'd ever returned his stolen gifts to?

"I don't think you'd better touch me. Or even… to be close to me. How do we know I won't go after you again?"

His lip curled in a smile. "I don't mind living dangerously. There isn't much in this world that poses a risk to me. It's rather… exciting."

Reg rolled her eyes. Trust Corvin to find everything about her attractive, even the danger. Did men ever grow out of wanting to tempt fate?

"I don't think it's a good idea. I think… everybody had better just stay away, until I get this sorted out."

"You don't want to live like a hermit. You've been fine up until now. I don't think you're suddenly going to start hunting anyone who comes by for a visit."

"Don't you?" Reg challenged.

"No." Corvin shook his head. "I don't."

"Well, you've got a lot more confidence than I do."

"I've studied more and lived more in the magical world than you have. I'm pretty confident that you will be able to stay in control. At least for the most part. And if you start behaving strangely, I'm on notice. I'll take off."

He wouldn't.

Reg grabbed Corvin's shoulders to pull him closer, and kissed him. He didn't even flinch. He didn't try to pull away or shake her off. He leaned in, sliding his hands around her. Reg pushed him back and jerked away.

"You're a liar!"

Corvin looked confused. Then it slowly dawned on him that it had been a test. She had been checking to see if he would retreat if she began to pursue. In the dim light from inside Reg's cottage, she could see him flush.

"I knew it wasn't the prelude to an attack."

"Right. How would you know that?"

"Because… you would…" He shook his head and shrugged. "We're not near the water. What point would there be in seducing me here?" He raised his eyebrows. "I mean… I can think of reasons, but not as part of an attack."

"You know better. You know Norma Jean charmed you at The Crystal Bowl, right there in the middle of town. And you know that she tried again here, to claim you and take you with her. So why wouldn't I?"

He gave off a very faint whiff of roses, quickly blown away in the evening breeze. He was too tired to charm her properly after their encounter on the beach.

"You're too weak."

His eyes slid away from her. He looked slightly chagrined at having failed to perform.

Reg opened her purse. Unlike her usual heavy shoulder bag, which contained everything but the kitchen sink, she'd only been able to fit a few small items into the tiny clutch purse. Finding her keys wasn't a problem. But that didn't mean she liked the little purse. It was cute, but she missed having her possessions with her. The security she felt at having her things close.

"Allow me," Corvin offered, reaching out to take the key from her and open her door. Reg jerked it back. She'd learned that lesson the hard way. Harrison had taught her all about the power that attached to keys. If she gave Corvin the key to open her door, it would defeat all of the wards of protection she had against him. And she wasn't about to do that again.

Reg fit the key into the lock, trying to keep an eye on him at the same time. But she wasn't as nervous of him as she would normally have been. She knew he was in a weakened state and still confused by what had happened. They both needed some time to think about it. To work out what it meant.

"Goodnight."

Corvin reached out and touched her neck and jaw just below her ear. It still sent lightning bolts of electricity charging through her. "Goodnight, Reg."

She pulled back from his touch and quickly entered the cottage. Once she was over the threshold, she felt a bit of a letdown. She knew that she was safe from him, and that now he would go home. Part of her wanted to let him in. To continue the dance between them and see where it would lead.

But she already knew where it would lead. And she wasn't about to let him drain her powers and leave her an empty husk.

Not again.

She was strong, and that wasn't going to happen again.

"You won't go to bed right away?" Corvin asked, before Reg shut the door.

"I don't know yet."

"You won't. You'll still stay up a few more hours."

"What difference does it make?"

"I'll be thinking about you. Maybe I'll call you."

"Don't. Leave me alone tonight. I need to think… all about this."

"I can help with research." He smiled, leaning closer to the opening in the door. "Try some experiments."

"Go away."

"I am serious, though," Corvin said, the smile disappearing. "Let me help you. We can work this out together."

Reg shook her head. There was something wrong with him, to still be attracted to her when he knew she had tried to drown him. And something wrong with Reg that she was still attracted to him.

She closed the door and bolted it.

CHAPTER SEVENTEEN

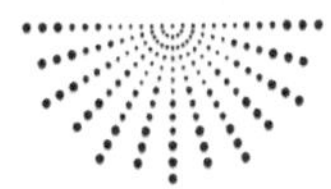

When she turned around, Starlight was sitting behind her. He was tall and thin, as if he'd been stretched like toffee. He blinked at her, watching her every move.

"What's wrong. Are you hungry?"

Reg moved toward the fridge, but Starlight didn't break his gaze. He kept watching her.

"We had ribs tonight," Reg told him. "I should have brought some home. Though they all had sauce and spices on them, and those things aren't very good for your digestion."

Even when she opened the fridge door, he still didn't start meowing and wrapping himself around her legs. Reg took out a takeout container of chicken and put it on the counter.

"Is something wrong? Are you sick?"

Norma Jean had done something to make him sick before, and now he was paying no attention to food. Did he sense that she was a siren too, and something about that had taken away his appetite? Could he sense that she'd tried to pull Corvin into the ocean, under the waves, where she could be alone with him and still be unafraid?

Reg swallowed.

"What is it, Starlight? Don't look at me like that."

He finally broke eye contact and looked toward the door.

"Is that it, you're just mad that I was out with Corvin?"

He meowed at her, a low note of agreement.

"Everything was fine. He didn't get into my head. He didn't steal any of my powers. Just the opposite—I—"

Her words dried up. She didn't know what she wanted to tell Starlight, how she would explain what she had tried to do. She felt powerful, knowing that she had nearly overcome Corvin, and could have if she hadn't fought herself. But that was sick. Not something she should have been proud of. Not something that Starlight would be proud of.

She swore under her breath and started to pull apart one of the drumsticks to feed the meat to Starlight.

He gave up on being tall and stern like an Egyptian cat statue and meowed for his supper. He rubbed against her legs, letting her know that all was forgiven. But would he forgive her if he knew what she had done? What she had tried to do?

* * *

Starlight had eaten and was sitting beside Reg on the couch. She petted him and closed her eyes, thinking over the evening. Somehow, evenings with Corvin always turned out to be way more challenging and eventful than they should. There were no quiet nights out with Corvin. She was just going to have to accept that.

"I should just stay away from him," she told Starlight. "Or he should stay away from me. I shouldn't have said yes to him. I don't owe him anything. We don't need to have any more dates."

Starlight purred loudly.

"You're not supposed to agree quite so fast."

"Humans are confusing."

Reg jumped, and looked around for the source of the voice.

She hadn't seen Harrison for some time, not since Yule. She hadn't called him during that time, but it still surprised her that he hadn't been around. Maybe she *should* have called him. Maybe he would have healed Calliopia for her without them having to go all the way to the mountains to have the blade unmade. Or maybe she should have called him to ask about Jacky Lane. But if she, a human, had problems understanding Jacky's motivations and behavior, then how was an immortal like Harrison going to unpack it?

"Harrison."

He sat in one of the wicker chairs, one long, skinny leg up over the arm like a teenager lounging. He was wearing all black, including a floppy-brimmed black hat, and looked something like a demented Zorro. Without a mask.

"What are you doing here?"

"Checking in on my goddaughter."

"You're not really my godfather. Or my uncle."

He shrugged. "That makes no difference."

"I suppose you know all about what went on tonight."

He arched an eyebrow. "I was trying to figure it out from what you said to Starlight, but…"

Starlight jumped down from the couch and marched over to Harrison, who instantly picked him up and began to stroke and cuddle him, making a low purring noise himself.

"Oh, good grief. The way the two of you go on." Reg shook her head and looked away from them, embarrassed by a grown man—or something that took the form of a grown man—being so silly over a cat. "I think the two of you must have been lovers in a previous life."

Harrison chuckled. "We all play many roles in many lives," he said obliquely. "One never knows."

"For once, could you say something that didn't sound like it came out of a fortune cookie?"

Harrison frowned, his brows bunching together, as he considered the question. Eventually, he shook his head. "No."

"It was a rhetorical question."

"Rhetorical."

"That means one you weren't supposed to answer, because I already know the answer. It's implied in the question."

He considered this. "Now you sound like a fortune cookie."

"It's your influence. That's what happens when I'm around you."

He smiled and nodded happily. "Good."

"No. Not good. Because I want answers."

"Then you should not... ask questions rhetorical."

"Ugh." Reg tried to shake off the confusion he always inspired. "I'm glad you're here tonight because I have some questions."

"Unrhetorical?"

"Unrhetorical."

Harrison put Starlight down in his lap and kept patting him.

"Did you know that Norma Jean was part siren?" Reg demanded.

He gave an easy nod.

"Why didn't you tell me that?"

"You did not know?"

"No. How could I know?"

Harrison pursed his lips.

"No." Reg waved her hand. "Don't answer that one. So if she is part siren, then so am I."

He tilted his head to the side. "That is likely," he agreed.

"Only likely? I inherited it from her, didn't I?"

He wobbled his hand back and forth. "Perhaps."

Maybe because Norma Jean was only part siren, Reg could have inherited the non-siren part. Or maybe, in the less-conventional way immortals produced offspring, Reg might not have inherited anything from Norma Jean. She could have nothing of either of them.

But Reg knew that wasn't true. She knew what had just happened.

"I guess that... I did inherit some of her siren genes. I don't want that to be true, and I said it wasn't, but..."

"Humans do not choose their physical forms."

It was a basic truth that Reg already knew, but when Harrison said it, it sounded inspired. And it sounded like he forgave her for whatever her physical nature was. Reg felt reassured for the first time. She hadn't done anything wrong. Or she didn't exist as something wrong. She was what she had been made.

"No. I didn't choose to be part siren."

Harrison nodded his agreement.

"But... I am. And now I don't know what to do about it."

"You cannot change what you are."

"Right. But what *can* I change or control? I don't have to… act like a siren, do I?"

"How does a siren not act like a siren? However a siren acts is how a siren is."

"Umm… yeah, I guess. But this siren doesn't want to… well… drown men."

"Ahh." Harrison nodded wisely. He looked toward the kitchen. "They don't… taste so good."

Reg's startled giggles were so high they were almost ultrasonic. She felt giddy. Maybe a little hysterical. Men didn't taste good? That was the best reason Harrison could think of not to kill them?

"I meant… I don't want to kill anything. I just want to live like the other normal humans. No siren nature. No taking men away and trying to drown them. Whether I eat them or not, it's wrong."

Harrison nodded sagely. He looked toward the kitchen again.

"Are you hungry?" Reg asked in exasperation.

"Do you have pizza?"

"No, I don't think so… if I do, it's probably old and gross." She really should clean out the fridge sometime before Sarah did. They were Reg's leftovers, or mostly so, and she should be the one responsible for cleaning up. "You should have seen the restaurant Corvin and I were at tonight. The best ribs you ever tasted!"

"Human ribs?"

"No! No, I'm not talking about eating human ribs. I'm talking about ribs… pork, I guess. We went to Uncle Mike's, and they have the best ribs you ever tasted."

"The best?" Harrison repeated.

Reg thought that he must have had ribs sometime in his immortal life. How could he go for hundreds or thousands of years without tasting ribs?

"Yes. You really have to try them—"

She should have known better than to say something like that. Harrison stood up and walked to Reg's kitchen, where the counters were suddenly covered with barbecue ribs on various platters and plates. Harrison put Starlight down on the island. He put on an Uncle Mike's bib. Starlight immediately started sniffing the various different plates. He sneezed at the spices on one. Harrison started picking up random ribs to taste, giving little bits to Starlight. He nodded and spoke through mouthfuls of food.

"Yes," he agreed, "they are much better."

Reg was afraid to ask what kind of ribs he had eaten in the past. Something prehistoric? Raw? Human? She was glad that he liked Uncle Mike's ribs, but she wondered how he had produced them. Had he made them out of thin air? Or had he transported them from Uncle Mike's? Were all of the cooks and waiters staring at empty counters and tables, wondering where the heck all of the ribs had suddenly disappeared to?

"So, can you help me?" she asked Harrison.

He gestured to the bounty on her counter. "Help yourself."

"No, I don't mean that. I had enough ribs. I'm not hungry. I meant… can you help me with not acting like a siren? With making sure that I don't… try to drown anyone?"

"If you do not want to, then do not."

"It's not that easy. I didn't want to tonight, but I was trying to capture Corvin and drag him into the ocean…"

"But you did not."

"No."

He made a motion toward her like she had proven his point.

"But I'm worried it might happen in the future. What if I'm too tired to be able to stop myself? What if I… do it in my sleep? Or in a trance? Norma Jean didn't really know what she was doing, not in the beginning, anyway."

"Norma Jean is what she is, and Reg Rawlins is not Norma Jean."

"I know." Reg huffed in frustration. "I didn't feel like I was in control. Something else was controlling me. This… hunger from deep down inside."

"Eat more ribs."

"It wasn't that kind of hunger."

"Then eat something else."

Reg stopped trying to explain and just watched him and Starlight as they ate the ribs.

CHAPTER EIGHTEEN

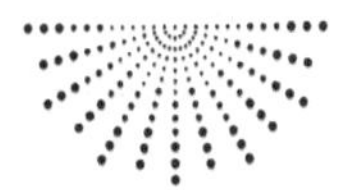

Reg wasn't sure when she had fallen asleep. She wasn't sure if Harrison had still been there, and if she had just nodded off or whether he had tucked her in, as he had sometimes before. Starlight lay cuddled up against her, apparently sleeping off his feast of ribs, late into the morning, long past when he usually would have insisted it was time for them to get up. Harrison had probably kept him up visiting.

"Does he make any more sense to you than he does to me?" Reg asked.

Starlight made a noise in his sleep but didn't open his eyes.

Reg looked around for her phone. It was on her bedside table, plugged into the charging cord. She must have put it there herself. She couldn't imagine Harrison being aware that phones had to be plugged in.

Reg grabbed it and unplugged it. She had a vague recollection of texting with Corvin. Had she?

She checked her notifications, but rather than seeing a new text from Corvin, she saw a series of voicemail messages and texts from Vivian King.

Reg let out her breath.

In all that had happened the night before, she had completely forgotten about her client's troubles. She should have followed up with Vivian before going to bed. At least shown that she had heard what happened and felt sympathy for Vivian. Instead, she'd been off on a date, and then talking with her… immortal godfather, if that's how he wanted her to think of him.

Reg skimmed over the texts and voicemail transcriptions, but she couldn't concentrate on the words. She would get up-to-speed better by talking to Vivian. She tapped one of the voicemails and tapped again to call back. The phone rang quite a few times and she didn't think Vivian was going to answer. Then there was a click.

"Reg?"

"Vivian. Hi. Sorry to be so long in getting back to you."

"Well, I guess you were probably sleeping. Sort of rude of me to think I can have your attention any time I want."

But the way she said it didn't make Reg think Vivian was sorry for calling at an inconvenient time. She felt that Reg shouldn't be sleeping when Vivian needed her.

Reg's foster families had always tried to get her to sleep on a normal schedule like normal people, insisting that if she were to be part of the real world and to be a productive member of society, she needed to sleep when they said she should.

And Reg never had. Try as she might, she couldn't get to sleep before the wee hours of the morning, and then her body wanted to sleep until noon. And despite what the many families had preached, that was perfectly okay. Not everybody slept at the same time. People worked night shift. There were plenty of people in Black Sands who stayed up late to make their potions and work their spells. Many of Reg's clients wanted to do seances, and those always worked better after dark, as close to midnight as possible. They couldn't expect her to be up again at six if she had been doing seances and readings until three o'clock in the morning.

"I had a late consulting job," Reg told Vivian. A half-truth. She *had* been consulting with Harrison, trying to sort out her new problem. Even if he hadn't come up with a solution for her, that didn't change the fact that she had been trying to work out her problems with him.

"So… I guess you didn't hear about what happened."

Reg feigned ignorance. "What happened?"

"I had… an incident. You remember how when you read the tea leaves for me, you saw those three images…"

"I thought you didn't think those images meant anything."

"I didn't. I thought you were just giving random images and hoping that I would connect them together later on, and then I would think that you had predicted the future. Because that's the way people think."

"So did you want to come for another reading? The crystal ball worked a lot better for you."

"Uh… no. I just wanted to tell you…"

Reg waited. Maybe it was a little mean to make Vivian come out and tell her what had happened, rather than letting her off the hook and saying she had seen it on TV. But she wanted Vivian to admit that Reg had been right, and they hadn't just been three random images that she'd hoped Vivian would be able to tie together.

"You see, there's this big tree outside my house," Vivian explained. "Or, the house that I'm renting. A big old tree. And yesterday… a big branch broke off of the tree…"

"Oh, that's too bad," Reg said blandly.

"It came in through my window. Crashed in through the kitchen window and sliding doors. It was huge. And…"

Reg waited.

"Well, I guess that's why you saw the tree, and house, and kitchen. Because that's exactly what happened."

"You could string any three random images together," Reg reminded her. "People's brains make connections, even where there aren't any."

"I don't think that these images just happened to be connected…"

"So…?"

"Well, I was wondering if you could help me. I thought… maybe if I tell you a little more, you can look into your crystal ball, and you could help me, or point me in the right direction to get help…"

"With what?"

"I'll explain when I get there…"

Reg was curious as to what Vivian would have to tell her. It was clear that a lot was going on that Vivian wasn't telling her. People didn't just have bad luck like Vivian did. There was something else going on.

* * *

Reg watched the trees waving out the window, watching for some sign of Forst, who she knew was there. But she often couldn't see him when he was working; he blended in with the garden so well. One wouldn't have thought that the red cap could just disappear into all of that green, but somehow it did.

There was a knock on the door, and Reg turned toward it and stood up. She walked to the door and opened it for Vivian.

Vivian stood there, looking just as she had the first day she had come to Reg. Not a mark on her from either the truck accident or the tree through the window. She had miraculously escaped injury in both cases. Reg wondered whether she had supernatural powers. Something that allowed her to move at the last moment when she was a split-second away from being crushed by a boulder, truck, or tree.

Vivian didn't just have bad luck; Reg was sure of that. There was something else going on.

"Hi, Vivian, come on in."

Reg had the tea made and out on the coffee table already. Vivian was right on time, so the water was piping hot and ready to go. Reg resumed her previous seat. Starlight jumped up onto the couch next to her and sat, looking at Vivian.

Vivian chose one of the chairs and sat down. She eyed Starlight. "You can see, sometimes, why cats were worshiped in ancient cultures."

Reg looked over at Starlight, the way he was sitting up tall, looking very regal. As if they were his servants. And she supposed she was. She made sure that he was fed, finding him special delicacies when he refused to eat the food that she had spent good money on, scooped his poop, cuddled with him, and kept him company. She'd taken him to the vet and strengthened him with her powers when he was sick, determined to find someone or something that could heal him. She'd found Nicole for him after he'd spotted her through the window. She was there to serve his every whim.

"I suppose so," she agreed. "They do manage to get under our skin. Corvin says that people domesticated them because they were helpful in catching mice. But I think cats domesticated people because they didn't want to waste all of their time catching mice."

Vivian laughed. "Yes, you're probably right about that one. They do seem to have us very well-trained."

Reg petted Starlight. She scratched his ears and gave him long strokes down the back.

"He's great when I do a reading. He helps me to focus my powers and… sort of magnifies the effect. It makes a big difference."

"He reminds me of Bastet."

Reg nodded. "Was that your cat…?"

Vivian laughed. "No. Bast. Bastet. She was an Egyptian god. Or is. Whatever."

Reg looked at Starlight. "Did you hear that? She just compared you to a god. I'll bet that makes you feel special."

Starlight just kept looking at Vivian, not at Reg. His ears flicked, but otherwise he was still. Like he was pretending to be one of those Egyptian statues. The regal Bastet.

He seemed fascinated by Vivian but, other than that, she wasn't able to sense any emotions from him. Was he keeping them from her? Or maybe she was just tired.

"So, you had something to tell me? I'm not sure what it is we're doing this session."

"Well…" Vivian delayed by pouring herself tea. She fussed with it, stirring, adding honey, considering the cream. "It's hard to know where to start. You know about Colorado. And about the truck and the tree."

"Francesca did say that bad luck comes in threes. So you should be off the hook for a few years now!"

Francesca shook her head. "I only wish that were the case."

Reg sipped her own tea, watching Starlight, waiting. Vivian

wanted to get it off her chest. Sooner or later, she was going to have to just come out with it.

"A lot of things like that have happened to me. And it seems like it's been getting worse. It used to be just occasional… bizarre, unlucky accidents. But it's like it's accelerating. Intensifying."

"So it didn't start with the house in Colorado?"

Vivian shook her head. "No. There were other things before that… and since then."

Reg leaned back, thinking about that. She picked Starlight up and held him in her lap. She closed her eyes and thought about the emotions around Vivian. Her aura.

"Is that why you were so worried about the black cats at Francesca's?"

"I don't know why I would worry about a little thing like that." Vivian shook her head. "I've already got more than my share of bad luck; it isn't like one black cat is going to change that."

Reg didn't correct her that there had been four black cats. Vivian had made her point. Why worry about cats when she had boulders crushing her house and runaway trucks making straight for her?

"So you're not worried about black cats."

"A little," Vivian sighed. "I'm kind of paranoid about anything that is supposed to cause bad luck. But it isn't like avoiding those things is going to change anything now."

"When did this bad luck start?"

"It's not just bad luck… I don't have trouble getting a job, or having to pay unexpected overage fees on my cell phone, or things like that. I've even tried buying lottery tickets, and I can still win the prizes, if I buy enough cards. It isn't bad luck; it's these accidents. These… near-death events."

"And it started…?"

"I don't know." Vivian thought back. She closed her eyes, and her face relaxed as she accessed her memories, trying to identify when the accidents had begun. "I was still pretty young… I was camping with my family. We did that kind of thing a lot. Went interesting places and camped out while we explored them. I was attacked by a lion. It got into the tent and dragged me off."

Reg leaned forward, her jaw dropping open in shock. She couldn't think of what to say. It was one thing to calmly talk about boulders rolling down the mountain to crush Vivian's house. But the thought of her as a little girl, being attacked by a lion…?

"That's horrible. You must have been terrified. What happened? How did you get away? Were you injured?"

"I woke up. I was screaming, writhing, trying to get away from it and figure out where I was and what was happening. My dad, he came out of the tent yelling, waving his arms around, and attacked the lion. He kept hitting it in the face with the heel of a shoe. And then… it dropped me, and ran away."

Reg blew out her breath. "Wow. That's incredible. And were you hurt?"

"No." Vivian's voice was low. "I got away without a scratch."

"That's amazing. And things like this have been happening ever since?"

"Yes."

"Attacked by a lion! You hear stuff like that every now and then in the news, but I never met anyone it happened to."

"People usually don't believe me."

"Really?" Reg thought about that, then nodded. "Yeah, I suppose. People never believed the stories I told as a kid." And with good reason. If someone didn't believe in her gifts, then they wouldn't believe the things that happened to her or around her.

"What about as an adult?"

Reg raised her brows. "I learned to tell more believable stories. Even if they weren't true."

Vivian nodded. "Yes. Exactly. People say they want to hear the truth, but they don't. They want to hear things they believe."

Starlight rubbed against Reg's chin and kneaded her legs, his sharp claws pricking her skin. "Ouch. Settle down." She scratched his chin and tried to get him to be still. "And… you think it's getting worse."

"It is. I used to have time between. Things would only happen every now and then. I had time… to have a life in between. To forget about it."

And now, things were apparently happening every day or two. "So what do you want me to do? You want me to… warn you what's going to happen next? Or something else?"

Vivian rubbed her teacup as if it had smudges on it, but Reg knew it didn't. "Knowing what's going to happen next doesn't seem to matter. Nothing I do seems to have any effect on the outcome."

Reg nodded. Despite her warnings about the truck and the house, those things had still happened. Vivian had avoided being killed. But if things like that had been happening ever since Vivian was a little girl, then she had already grown pretty adept at avoiding death. While Reg had initially thought that Vivian must be the unluckiest woman in the world, she had to wonder whether Vivian was actually the luckiest. How else had she avoided being killed?

"So… what, then? I'm not sure what you want me to do for you."

"I was hoping… that you might be able to do something to figure out why this is happening to me. What I can do to make it stop. I just want to end… these accidents."

"Well… I'm not sure I can do anything about that. I'll try to figure out why, but that's not really my wheelhouse. You have a bit of time?"

"Where am I going to go? If I leave here, something bad is just going to happen. Tonight, tomorrow… I don't know when, but something is going to happen."

"And you don't know why it's happening? There's nothing… that you've done in your past…?"

She was thinking of Jacky and the spirits that had attached to her. The things that had happened to her had been karmic. The ghosts' anger, restlessness, and in the end, retribution, had been fully justified. Jacky might have thought it unfair that she had to pay for her crimes, but Reg couldn't argue with what had happened.

"I did something?" Vivian demanded. "You think that a little girl did something that justifies all of this bad stuff that has happened to me? If I did something awful, it's been paid for ten times over. I just want to… I want to live out a normal life. I want this all to end."

"Sometimes people have some idea of why things are happening. It's worth asking."

"The answer is no. I didn't do something to deserve this," Vivian said petulantly.

"Okay. Do you mind if I use the crystal ball? That seemed to work well the first time."

Vivian nodded. "Whatever would give you the clearest answer. Of course. I want to know. I want some progress. I can't go on living like this."

Reg nodded. She had already put the crystal ball out on the coffee table, assuming that she would be using it at some point. So she didn't have to dislodge Starlight in order to get up and place it where she could see into it.

She gazed at the crystal, initially looking deep into the depths of the glass, and then defocusing her eyes and just looking at its fuzzy, blurred shape. She buried her fingers in Starlight's fur, kneading his muscles and waiting for some insight.

CHAPTER NINETEEN

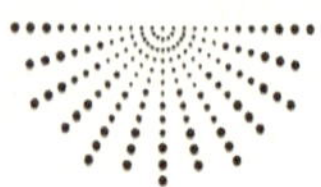

For a long time, she just sat there, waiting for something to happen. Usually, she could see the future pretty quickly, or view something remotely. She'd had trouble with seeking objects ever since she had been injured with Calliopia's magical knife, and subsequently healed. She'd hoped that with Calliopia performing a severance spell, and later with the unmaking of the blade, that her ability to seek would have returned, but she still had to work very hard to see anything she was looking for. Unless it were Calliopia herself.

Maybe seeing why Vivian's life was so dangerous was something that was beyond her powers. Seeing the past was harder for Reg than seeing the future. And maybe seeing someone else's past was beyond her abilities, however much she had grown and advanced.

"Can you touch the ball?" Reg invited. "Just put your fingertips on the crystal."

Vivian sat still at first, then reluctantly moved to do as Reg had asked. She extended her fingers as if she were going to touch a hot pan. Ready to jerk them back the instant she felt the heat. Was she that worried about seeing the past? Or was it something else?

Reg's head immediately began to clear. She closed her eyes for a few moments, breathing and focusing, then opened them again to peer into the glass.

At first, it was dark. Not just empty, without anything visible in the crystal, but black, filled with a thick, dark fog. Reg waited. It wasn't nothing. It was something. So she was prepared to wait and see what it became.

Vivian was breathing shallowly, looking down at the crystal ball. Reg wondered whether she could see the darkness, or whether for her, the crystal was just as blank and empty as ever. She didn't dare ask and break their concentration.

The fog cleared slowly. It didn't blow away like it might on some TV movie, gone in a puff so that they could see what lay beneath. Instead, it just thinned gradually, becoming less opaque. More transparent. Reg observed, still scratching Starlight's ears and kneading his muscles, using his psychic powers, her own, and Vivian's own strength and experience to uncover the reasons behind Vivian's bad luck.

Eventually, she saw a little girl, dark-skinned, black-haired, lying in a coarse-looking tent, her eyes closed in sleep. Others lay around her, a communal sleeping tent. Her parents, she assumed, maybe Vivian's brothers and sisters or household servants or guides. Vivian hadn't spoken of any siblings, but that hadn't been relevant to her story. It wasn't about anyone else; it was just about her.

There were noises in the night around them—animal sounds, people in other tents or shacks that were close. Reg could smell wood smoke, fragrant and a little pungent. Food smells. Someone had cooked recently. Maybe there was still a rabbit or some other meat on a spit nearby.

There was a growling and snuffling. Ominous footsteps padding nearer and nearer, loud in the stillness of a night without the sound of any cars or planes or all-night bars.

Reg knew a split-second before it happened what she was going to see. The cat burst in, not through the flap of the tent, but right through the side, ripping the fabric aside as if it were nothing more than a mirage, and clamped its jaws over the little girl's head.

The girl let out a shriek, not even fully awake, and started to thrash around. The lion kept its grip on her head and started to back away, retreating to where it could deal with her alone. The others in the tent were slow to awaken. Maybe they'd had a busy day and were worn out. Maybe they'd been drinking. Or maybe there was supposed to be a night watchman, so the others had gone to sleep thinking they did not need to be wary and listen for trouble.

Then a man squirmed out of the collapsed tent. His face was darker than Vivian's and difficult to make out in the dimness of the night. There were no lights, just the moon and the stars.

The man chased after the lion, yelling, trying to frighten it into dropping its prey. Behind them, a woman started to cry and shriek. The mother, putting together what had happened and realizing that her child was gone.

The man clubbed the lion furiously. It turned and tried to bite him, but to do so, had to release its prey. The man moved fast, pounding his makeshift club, a large boot, into the lion's face over and over again, aiming for its eyes, ears, and tender nose.

The big cat dropped the little girl, tried once or twice to retaliate and bite or claw the man, then began to retreat. The man started to yell in a language that Reg didn't understand, calling the others in the camp to him to help. A few brave souls banded together to chase the retreating wildcat, while others formed a circle around Vivian, looking at the state of the child, chanting, watching for any other lions. A big male like the one that had attacked Vivian wouldn't usually do his own hunting, leaving it to the lionesses, but this rogue must have been a bachelor, a young lion who didn't yet have a pride of his own. But they kept their eyes open anyway. They could be wrong and there might still be a lioness or two close by, watching for their chance to make off with the little girl or with another child left unattended in the general confusion.

The child Vivian cried softly, probably in shock, not yet sure what had happened to her. The others in the camp would tell her about it, providing the details she needed to build a complete picture. She would grow up knowing that she was the child who had escaped the lion's teeth.

The man scooped her up and held her close. His body was hot and sweaty, his breath rotten, and he had a few cuts on his face and body that oozed blood, but Vivian clung to him, holding on for dear life, terrified in the darkness and needing the comfort of his familiar form.

He spoke in a tongue Reg didn't understand, soothing Vivian gently, bouncing her. He stroked her hair and told her with loud, wide vowels what had happened to her, how she had escaped the lion that had tried to steal her away. She pressed her face into the hollow of his neck, not crying, but still and scared, trying to process it all.

Reg closed her eyes. It was the story that Vivian had already told her. Interesting to see, but not providing any more enlightenment into why this streak of bad luck had begun. She needed to go farther back. The lion wasn't the beginning. Maybe it was the first in a long series of misfortunes, but it wasn't the trigger. Something had happened to start the dominoes falling in the first place.

Reg waited, focused on the past. Before the lion attack. Something had happened before.

CHAPTER TWENTY

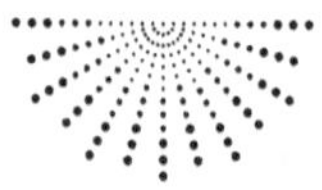

There was a knock on the door, and then Sarah was opening it and walking in, already chattering away to Reg. It wasn't until she was halfway to the kitchen that she realized her mistake, processing that Reg was sitting with a client in mid-reading.

"Oh, no! I'm so sorry! I didn't know you had a guest."

Reg realized belatedly that she hadn't bothered to give Sarah a heads-up. Maybe she needed to start an online booking calendar that either of them could see so that they didn't have to physically go to the counter to look at it or call to let the other know there had been a recent addition. But Reg wasn't very good at keeping a calendar. She always had the best of intentions. It didn't seem like a difficult thing, making sure to enter each new commitment into her phone. But in reality, her brain just didn't work that way. She needed to see the appointment book on the counter, to have it constantly there in front of her every time she walked by or went into the kitchen to get something to eat. She needed to physically turn the pages and see what was written there. With an online calendar, it was too easy to forget, look at the wrong day, or get confused over the tiny, cramped lines.

The vision was gone. The crystal ball was clear once more. Vivian drew back, removing her fingers and looking at the newcomer.

"I forgot to let you know," Reg reassured Sarah. "It was sort of last minute, and I forgot to tell you someone would be coming over."

She motioned to Vivian.

"Sarah, this is Vivian. Vivian, Sarah."

The women nodded and greeted each other politely. Sarah was studying Vivian closely, a frown on her face.

"Vivian is new in town," Reg advised, hoping to help Sarah to make the connections. "She was just looking for a reading."

Vivian looked at Sarah. Sarah looked back.

"Maybe you saw Vivian on the news?" Reg suggested. "She had an accident…"

"Yes, I'm sure that was it," Sarah murmured. But her tone was not convincing.

"I need to go," Vivian said, looking down at her wrist.

She had said only moments before that she had as long as it took for Reg to find out what was going on. But maybe she had decided that Reg wasn't going to be able to. Reg slid her phone out of her skirt pocket and looked at it. She was surprised by how much time had passed. It had seemed like Vivian had only been there for a few minutes, but hours had passed. Had they been looking into the crystal ball the whole time? And if so, had Vivian seen what Reg had seen? Or had she seen something different? Or nothing at all?

"If you could stay for just a few more minutes…" Reg suggested. "Sarah doesn't need me right now. We'll talk later."

Vivian looked over at the older woman, uncertain. Sarah nodded slowly. "Yes, it's my fault for busting in without checking first. I'm sorry. I'll leave the two of you. Reg can get back to me at a more convenient time. In fact, there isn't really anything I need; I was just coming over to gossip and see if she needed anything."

Vivian stood. She looked at the door, then back at Reg. She wanted to escape, but she had asked for help and Reg wasn't finished with her.

Sarah walked back toward the door. "I'm sorry," she repeated. "I really didn't mean to interrupt you."

She left, pulling the door shut behind her. Vivian didn't sit back down.

"Maybe this wasn't such a good idea."

"I think we were making progress." Reg shifted Starlight onto the couch beside her and stood up as well, stretching her muscles. She had been sitting hunched over the crystal in one position for too long. She was tired and her mind was full of what she had experienced looking into the crystal ball, and she wouldn't be able to do another session even if Vivian stayed. "Can we talk for a minute and then maybe schedule a follow-up appointment?"

Vivian shifted awkwardly. "Yes, I suppose."

"I'm sorry about the interruption."

Vivian nodded.

"I don't know whether you were able to see what I saw in the crystal…? I know most people don't, but sometimes they catch glimpses."

"Glimpses," Vivian agreed. "Just an impression here and there… It was the lion, wasn't it? The lion that attacked me when I was little."

"Yes."

"Is that how it started, then? The lion… marked me somehow? Was it a magical creature? It didn't kill me, but the magic is still working in me…?"

"No…" Reg didn't think that was it, but she hadn't thought along those lines at all. "I think this might have been the first episode, but I don't think this is what caused your misfortunes."

"What, then?"

"That's why I would like to get together again. I think we're close. Maybe we would have been able to figure it out today if we hadn't been interrupted, but I don't think I can find my place again today. I need a break and some time to think about it. Can we meet again tomorrow?"

"Does it need to be tomorrow?"

"Oh… well, if you have something going on tomorrow, it could be the next day."

"No, no. I mean… could it be earlier? It's not that late. Maybe tonight sometime? You can relax for a while. I can go… get something to eat or do some shopping while you rest, and then I'll come back…"

"Sure." Reg nodded. She wasn't sure that it would be long enough, but Vivian was desperate. Things were happening to her at an increasing pace. She didn't feel like she could wait a whole day, and Reg respected that. She couldn't imagine what it would be like to have to face the disasters that Vivian had been dealing with on a daily basis. It was inconceivable. "Why don't we say… nine or ten tonight? Would that be okay?"

"That won't be too late for you?"

"I'm used to being up late. Midnight is better for seances and readings. That's why I didn't get back to you earlier today."

"Right. Of course. If that's okay with you, then. I'm sorry to be so pushy about it, but…"

"I understand. I get why you don't want to wait."

Vivian nodded. She rubbed the back of her head and let out a long sigh. "If we could at least identify why this is happening… I would be so grateful. Maybe then someone could help me to find a way to stop these accidents."

Reg wasn't sure how she was going to do that. But she had friends who might be able to advise or help her. At least point her in the right direction.

* * *

After Vivian left, Reg texted Sarah to let her know that she was gone, though she suspected that Sarah had probably been watching out the window and would already know. It was a few minutes before Sarah came over, still looking chagrined.

"I am so sorry, Reg. And you were right in the middle of a reading; it was obvious I completely derailed everything. I'd be happy to pay you for the session, and you can refund Vivian and get together with her again…"

"She's going to come back tonight. It's okay, really. I'm not sure how much more we could have gotten out of that session anyway."

"Are you sure? I didn't mean to interrupt."

"It's fine." Reg started to clear away the used teacups. "I got the feeling… you knew Vivian from somewhere."

Sarah didn't answer right away, frowning to herself.

"Didn't you?" Reg prompted.

"Well… she did remind me of someone. But that was so many years ago…"

Reg cocked her head, thinking about it. "Does that mean… she's a practitioner?" A lot of the witches and warlocks around Black Sands seemed to be much older than they looked because of their practice. But Vivian hadn't said that she was a practitioner. She had implied that she was just a regular mortal human who didn't know much about the practice of magic or about psychic gifts. Reg considered what that might mean in light of the vision in the crystal. Nothing had appeared until Vivian had touched the crystal. Could Reg trust what she had seen, or had Vivian planted it there? Verification of the story that she had already told Reg. The story that she had not expected Reg to believe.

"If it was her, then yes… but I suppose it could be her daughter or granddaughter. Some descendant who inherited many of her features…"

"The woman that you knew, what was her name?"

"Oh… I don't remember. We only met each other in passing; I don't think there were any formal introductions. It was a chaotic time…"

"Was she… good or bad?"

Reg knew that Sarah wouldn't like this. She liked to profess that there was no good or bad, no white or dark magic, just people and their practices. Choices. What worked and what didn't. But Reg's experience didn't align with that philosophy. Reg had met bad people. Evil people. Both humans without magic and those who had gifts. Some people, like Corvin, might be hard to classify, when they were sometimes helpful and sometimes predators, but that didn't mean that good and bad didn't exist.

"I couldn't tell you," Sarah said, her mouth squinched up like she'd tasted something sour. "I saw things… heard things… but you can't judge a person by gossip. You have to know them personally, close up. And I didn't know her. I was only… aware of her."

Which was entirely unhelpful. Reg didn't like to think that she might be helping someone who could be wicked. She didn't want to help an evil practitioner to grow in power. Maybe there was a reason bad things were happening to Vivian. Maybe, like with Jacky, it was karma. Bad things happening because she was doing harmful things herself.

"So you can't tell me anything more than that? You might have seen her or heard something about her years ago, and she might be that person or a descendant of that person."

"That's about the shape of it," Sarah agreed. "You see why I'm hesitant to say anything at all. It's all just holes and speculation."

Reg nodded. She sat back down with Starlight. "I'll just have to keep that in mind, then. That she might be a practitioner or the descendant of a practitioner. Should I assume that... she was pretty powerful? It seems like she wouldn't still be alive unless her powers were pretty strong."

"I don't know, Reg. I'm sorry. I'm less than useless in this matter."

Reg petted Starlight, thinking through what she knew.

CHAPTER TWENTY-ONE

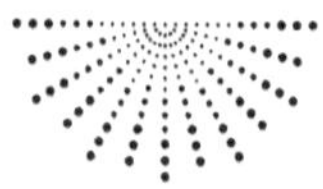

When Vivian returned, Reg couldn't help looking at her with a little more suspicion than she had previously.

She had, to begin with, taken Vivian at face value. A woman who had experienced a series of traumatic events, who was looking for some help from a psychic in order to sort things out and maybe find a way to put a stop to the disasters that followed her wherever she went. Now… she wasn't so sure. There was more to the story.

She didn't know what it was that Sarah knew or suspected. Sarah wasn't going to tell her. That might mean it was something bad, something that was taboo to talk about, or just that she didn't know anything.

Reg didn't quite believe that she didn't know anything.

Reg first studied Vivian's face. Her skin was dark and smooth, without a wrinkle. If she were a normal mortal human without any magical help, she could be anywhere from twenty to fifty. No gray hair, but hair was easily dyed.

She looked down at Vivian's hands. She knew from holding and reading many people's hands that it was easier to tell age from the hands than the face. People didn't go to the same lengths to keep them looking young. The hands could give a person away. But Vivian's hands also appeared ageless. Uncalloused, unwrinkled, no age spots or blemishes. Her fingers were long and tapered, palms lighter than the rest of her skin. Just as Reg would expect them to look. Was it a disguise? An immortal putting on human flesh? Some other species that looked human but wasn't? Reg was getting better at recognizing fairies and some of the other magical races, but she couldn't claim to be able to recognize them straight off, and she was sure there were some species that she hadn't yet encountered.

Or Vivian could be possessed by some other entity. There could be something completely foreign lurking underneath.

Vivian looked back at Reg, amusement in her eyes. "Do I pass your test?"

"I don't know," Reg confessed. "You seem real enough to me."

"I am real."

"And human? And… I don't know. Normal?"

"What else would I be? An alien? Normal, I don't know about. That's a little harder to classify. I don't think, with everything that has happened, that I can claim to be quite as normal as everyone else."

"Yeah." Reg was in the same boat. Normal was something she had left behind some time ago. "I know what you mean. Sorry, I'm just trying to get things straight in my mind. This isn't something you run into every day."

"I wouldn't guess so." Vivian rolled her eyes. "Can you imagine this being commonplace? All kinds of people like me running around?"

Disaster magnets every which way. No, that would not be good.

Which led to the question of why Vivian? And why was it getting worse, as if fate were more and more determined to remove her from the world?

"Let's sit down."

They resumed their seats of earlier in the day.

"You're feeling better?" Vivian asked. "You're… strong enough? Focused enough?"

Reg had rested and slept. She'd fortified herself with a quick drink before Vivian had arrived. It probably wouldn't help with her focus, but she hoped it would steady her nerves.

"Yeah. It's closer to midnight too, which sort of... opens some doors. The veil gets thinner."

Vivian seemed uninterested in the details.

Reg rubbed her palms on her skirt and focused on the crystal ball. Starlight was sleeping in the bedroom. Hopefully, the hour would work in their favor and she wouldn't need him.

"What else do you remember about the vacation when you were attacked by the lion?"

"It wasn't a vacation," Vivian objected. "We traveled around a lot."

"I thought you said you were camping."

"Yes. But that's what we did. We were... nomadic. We would go somewhere new, and we would camp while we explored the area. My dad would find work in one of the villages, maybe." She blinked, thinking about it. "He was... sort of an archaeologist."

"So what else do you remember about it? About that place in particular?"

Vivian squinted off into the distance and rubbed her forehead, thinking about it. "There was a dig site nearby. I remember going there with my parents. They gave me a little shovel and let me dig my own site. I copied what they did." She shrugged.

"That sounds like fun."

"I was very serious about it, wanting to be like the grown-ups. But I got bored easily."

"Sure, of course." Reg waited for more from Vivian. "So... did anything strange happen while you were there? Any accidents or problems other than the lion's attack?"

"No, I don't think so." Vivian pondered this. "I quite liked it there, other than the lion attack. My father found a lot of artifacts so we were able to live comfortably."

"In tents?" Reg was skeptical.

Vivian laughed. "Nomadic tribes all over the world have been living in tents for hundreds and thousands of years. Some of them are quite lavish. Big multi-room tents in compounds or villages, lots of furs and blankets to keep warm and cushion your bones from the ground, fires and guards to keep away the wildlife."

"Mostly."

Vivian nodded and shrugged. "Mostly," she agreed. "I don't think you can really judge from my experience. If you did, you wouldn't think that houses were safe to live in either, would you?"

Considering that Vivian had lived in one house that had been crushed by a boulder and another that had been invaded by a tree, she had a point. And there were house fires, earthquakes, tornadoes, and other human-made or natural disasters that destroyed houses every year. Even knowing that, Reg felt perfectly safe in her little cottage.

"I guess you're right," she agreed. "I can't judge by one little lion attack."

Vivian chuckled. "I'm surprised you even believe me. It isn't like I have any scars to prove my story. Most people seem to think I'm just making it up."

"But I saw it in the glass." Reg motioned to the crystal ball that she was still keeping an eye on. "I saw it there with my own eyes."

The other woman gave a shrug that suggested she still didn't quite believe in what Reg might have seen in the orb. Reg could be making it up. She *had* predicted the truck accident, which should have been proof enough of her psychic abilities. But she could be making up what she had seen of the lion attack. Vivian had said that she'd caught glimpses of it herself, but people generally talked themselves out of such things after a while. It would be easy for Vivian to say that it was the power of suggestion, that she hadn't really seen anything in the crystal ball, she had just remembered bits and pieces of the attack with a few well-placed suggestions or a hallucinogenic substance added to the tea.

Reg touched the side of the crystal ball with her right forefinger and middle finger. "Tell me what it was like there. Did you have brothers and sisters?"

"No, I was an only child. My parents probably didn't want to be dragging a whole brood around to these different archaeological sites. I don't know if they had even planned on me. I wouldn't be surprised if I was a mistake. They never told me that I was and they weren't abusive… I just don't think that a child fit in that well with their lifestyle."

Reg waited, trying to bring the vision of the lion back into the ball. It had been night. Desert. Dark. Dry.

She saw the flickering lights of fires and torches. It must have been a long time ago. If Sarah were right, and Vivian was a practitioner, then she might have been a child before the advent of electricity or, at least, the widespread adoption of electricity. Or they might just have had to 'rough it' when they were at an archaeological site. If there were no infrastructure and no generators, they would live more primitively.

"Where was this? I know it was desert. And we don't have lions like that in North America, unless it escaped from a zoo. That's not very likely, so…?"

"With some of the things that have happened to me, an escaped zoo animal would not be beyond the realm of possibility."

Reg waited. She had seen the other people who had been in the same camp or village as Vivian's family. They all had dark skin, and most of them had the type of clothing she associated with tribal people. They didn't look American, but maybe African or Australian.

"Northern Africa," Vivian confirmed Reg's guess. "We spent a lot of time in sites around there. It was very pleasant. Hot, yes, but children run and play in the heat and don't really notice it. Not when you grow up in it. Coming here to America, I found that very cold. My blood is still too thin."

"You probably like Florida better than Colorado."

"Oh, yes! Definitely!"

"I grew up in the north, so I understand how cold it gets. The winter…"

"The winter." Vivian shuddered. "Yes."

Reg tried to feel the sensations that she had felt when she saw the vision in the glass. She hadn't just seen what had happened, she had experienced it, as if she had been right there with Vivian. The grit on her skin. The smells and the sights. It had all been there, as if Vivian had implanted the whole experience in her brain.

"There were other children there? Were you afraid to go out after it had happened? You must have been traumatized."

"I don't think I was," Vivian said, her voice thoughtful. "It was scary, but I don't remember being afraid that it was going to happen again. My parents were very comforting about it; they said they would keep me safe. There were more guards. Hunting parties went out looking for the lion that had attacked me. I still went and played with the other children, dug in my little site, kept sleeping in the tent, all of that."

"And that was the only strange thing that happened there?" Reg pressed again. "No one died unexpectedly; your parents were still okay, all that?"

"Perfectly normal. That's really the only notable thing that happened."

"What was the next thing that happened? The next accident?"

"It's been so many years, and really, so many bizarre things have happened. It's hard to remember them all clearly."

"The next thing you remember."

"Well… I fell off a cliff."

Reg frowned at her. "Off of a cliff?"

"Another girl and I were playing around… jumping and wrestling and racing…" Vivian gave a wry smile.

"And you fell off of the cliff?"

"Yes. We ran into each other and I kind of bounced off of her and fell. All the way down."

Reg's heart sped up just thinking about it. "Down how far?"

"Uh… fifty feet? I don't know. I bounced off some scrub bushes." She gave a shrug. "I know… never should have survived."

"Good grief!" Reg shook her head. She didn't try to see the incident in the crystal ball. She didn't want to see the little girl plummeting down fifty feet. "How badly were you hurt?"

"Nothing major. I had a few cuts and bruises, but those were probably just from roughhousing, not necessarily the fall. We were being pretty wild, jumping and wrestling and crashing into each other."

"How could you survive something like that without any injuries?"

"They couldn't say. Sometimes it just happens. There was some case here in the States where a little girl fell down a hollow tree on her head, and instead of being killed or injured, it cured her incurable disease. Sometimes… truth is stranger than fiction. I'm not the only kid ever to inexplicably survive a falling over a cliff."

"So… what did your parents think about all of these things? They must have wanted to wrap you in bubble wrap."

"They were pretty calm about it. After the first few incidents, they kind of got used to the fact that no matter what horrible thing happened, I would be just fine, so they didn't worry about it."

"That would take a lot of faith." Reg couldn't imagine getting to the point where she didn't worry about what happened to her kids, and she didn't even have any.

"Or a lot of anxiety. I think that once you get to a certain point… a certain level of adrenaline and being worried all the time… your body decides that's enough, and reduces the response level."

"I don't know. I've dealt with a lot of anxiety, and it doesn't seem to go away just because it's repeated."

"But maybe you haven't been pushed to that level. That one that's just too much for your body."

Reg shrugged. "Maybe."

CHAPTER TWENTY-TWO

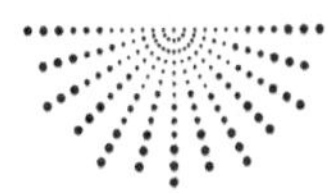

here was a knock at the door, and Reg and Vivian both looked toward it.

"Not again," Reg groaned. But the door was not opened by Sarah. Whoever had knocked was waiting for a response. "Sorry," Reg advised. "If this keeps up, I'm going to need a 'do not disturb' light outside my door, like at a radio station or psychiatrist's office."

Vivian leaned back and waited to see who was interrupting them this time. Reg heard Starlight jump to the floor, and he wandered out with an inquiring meow, headed toward the door to see who it was.

Reg eyed him to make sure he wasn't going to attempt escape. He'd only done it once before, but she didn't want him running out into the night. Anything could happen to him out there. He could get hit by a car or eaten by an alligator. Vivian's bad luck could attach to him and he could have a house dropped on him.

She opened the door and saw a tall, pale teen girl standing on her doorstep, arms folded across her chest while she waited impatiently. A short boy stood behind her, his brown curly hair and apple cheeks making him look about ten years old. But Reg knew them both, and neither was what they seemed. Calliopia was a fairy. Adolescent, but probably years older than Reg. And Ruan, for all of his prepubescent looks, was a full-grown pixie. Both had caused her considerable trouble in the past, but she couldn't help feeling a little responsible for them. What trouble were they in this time? They rarely came over for just a casual visit.

"Hi. What's up?"

"We saw Reg Rawlins' light was still on," Calliopia observed. "You are not sleeping."

"No. What are you doing out? How are you feeling?"

Calliopia was still recovering from a grave knife wound and wasn't yet up to traveling very far at a time. She put her hand on the door-frame and peered around Reg. "A guest?"

"Yes. I'm working. If you don't need anything, maybe we could talk tomorrow."

Starlight was creeping closer, his nose moving as he smelled the air. While fairies and pixies did not like cats, Ruan had come to appreciate Starlight's company and had taken to bringing him treats of spiders and other gross things Reg didn't want to know about. This time, though, he didn't take anything out of his pockets.

"We go soon," he informed Reg. "Will not be here much longer."

"Will you be here tomorrow?"

He exchanged a long look with Calliopia. "We know not."

Reg hesitated. She didn't want to interrupt another session with Vivian, but they weren't getting very far in unwinding the mystery behind Vivian's accidents, and Reg didn't want to send Calliopia and Ruan away with the possibility that she might never see them again. She was connected to Calliopia and wanted to know what was happening in her life. She hoped to be able to keep Calliopia out of trouble, so she didn't get hurt again.

"Well, come in, I guess. No tricks…"

Ruan shook his head. "Reg Rawlins always says no tricks," he said. "But that is not enough to stop Ruan Rosdew."

"No, I don't suppose it is."

She avoided looking in his eyes, though she was tempted to do so to check whether he was teasing her or he was actually planning on causing some kind of mischief. But looking in his eyes was just the opening he would need to mesmerize her and gain control over her. So she looked away, checking to make sure Starlight was still far enough away from the door. The pixie and the fairy entered. Calliopia seemed to be glowing slightly in the dimness of the room, lit only by lamps and candles. Her eyes swept the interior of the cottage, and she made her way to the couch, where she motioned for Ruan to sit down with her. Reg sat in the chair that was a mate for Vivian's. She tried to proceed without looking awkward.

"Uh, Vivian, this is Calliopia Papillon and Ruan Rosdew. They are… friends of mine. They're going to be leaving on a long trip soon, so I hope you don't mind them coming in for a short visit."

Vivian shrugged, looking over Calliopia and Ruan curiously. Had she ever seen a fairy or a pixie before? Or if she had, did she know what she had seen? They looked human enough, but their natures were quite different, and fairies and pixies didn't normally have anything to do with each other.

Calliopia shifted her position a few times, clearly still bothered by the wound in her side. But she was stronger and looked better than she had for a long time. Restless and impatient to hit the road again, pursuing the nomadic lifestyle that she and Ruan had been following until she was injured. Maybe the type of lifestyle that Vivian had known when she was young, moving frequently from place to place, settling in someplace new for a few weeks, then folding up the tent and going somewhere else.

Calliopia snagged the chain of her necklace with one finger and pulled the pendant out from her bosom, where it had settled inside her dress. She stroked it with her thumb, then eventually let it rest there where it was more visible and closer at hand when she felt the need to hold the talisman. Reg hadn't figured out yet whether it helped Calliopia's physical pain, or it was just a comfort to hold it in her hand, feeling the familiarity of the metal that had once been her favored dagger.

Vivian's eyes remained fixed on the pendant. She leaned a little closer to Calliopia. "It's a cat, isn't it? Can I see?"

Calliopia didn't move or answer. Undeterred, Vivian moved

closer, stepping around the coffee table so that she was only inches away from Calliopia's talisman, examining it closely.

At least she didn't touch it. Reg didn't think Calliopia would have countenanced that.

"It's beautiful," Vivian said, giving Calliopia a friendly smile. "I have one too."

And demonstrating, she pulled her own necklace out from under her blouse and dangled it in front where Calliopia could see it.

Calliopia's expression changed from disinterest to fascination. She too leaned in to get a better look at Vivian's pendant. Reg couldn't see it until Vivian turned around to face her, holding it so that Reg too could have a look.

Unlike the cat on Calliopia's pendant of fairy steel, which was sitting sedately looking back at the observer, Vivian had a gold pendant of a cat mid-leap or mid-run, body stretched out long in motion. It had the appearance of something ancient, formed by hands centuries ago. Reg wasn't sure whether it was supposed to represent a domesticated cat or some kind of panther or wildcat. The features were chunky and rough.

"Wow. Where did you get that?"

Vivian looked at Reg and didn't answer. Reg glanced over at Ruan and Calliopia, who were listening with interest. She realized that Vivian might not want to say too much in front of the strangers. And that would probably be wise, since Reg's next questions would have been whether it was real gold and what it was worth. Definitely not questions one should ask in front of potential thieves. Both the pixie and the fairy had been known to steal before. They felt justified in taking whatever they felt should be theirs. And things of value, especially that came out of the earth, would be of interest to both of them.

"That's very nice. I suppose it's probably been in your family for a long time." Reg tried to signal with her eyes that Vivian should put it away. Out of sight, out of mind, hopefully. She would do her best to get Ruan and Calliopia out of there so that she could ask Vivian more about her pendant.

"A cat. Is it a talisman?" Ruan demanded. "Has it magical protection?"

Vivian's brows went up. She sat back down in her chair. "Magical?" she asked with a tinkling laugh. "No. Of course not."

"Humans say cats are lucky, do they not?"

"Lucky?" Vivian shook her head. She held it in her hand for a moment, and then tucked it into her blouse again. "No. They're supposed to be bad luck. Especially black cats," she said, looking aside at Starlight.

"Black cats are not bad luck," Reg insisted, getting tired of this suggestion. "No cats are bad luck. Some cultures worship cats."

"Worship?" Ruan repeated. "Do they offer them on altars?"

"No." Reg told him firmly. She did not want this to lead to a conversation about cooking or eating cats. While Ruan was friendly with Starlight, that did not stop him from talking about how tasty cats were. "They made statues of them. Worshiped them and put them in tombs."

Her knowledge of such things was seriously lacking. Corvin would have known a lot more details. He was such a scholar about magic and other cultures. He didn't like cats either, but he would know about them.

"Cats were worshiped in Egypt," Vivian said. "Like Reg says. Humans probably domesticated small wildcats because they hunted mice around food stores. It was a mutually beneficial relationship. And as they became domesticated, they came to represent home and hearth. Safety, fertility, and motherhood." Her hand went to her pendant.

"What was the name of the one you were talking about before?" Reg asked. "You said that Starlight reminded you of him."

"Her. Bastet."

"Bastet." Reg pulled out her phone to look it up. "How do you spell that?"

"Just the way it sounds."

Reg tapped a couple of letters in, hoping that it would come up as a suggestion in her browser window. She looked at Vivian.

"B-A-S-T-E-T," Vivian dictated, her tone impatient.

Reg tapped it in. She looked at the pictures that came up, and then turned it around to show Calliopia and Ruan.

Ruan peered at the pictures. "These ones look like cats. But these are a woman with a cat's head." He shook his head. "What creature is a woman with a cat's head?"

"That's how they drew their cat god," Reg explained.

Ruan frowned, shaking his head again. He clicked his tongue at Starlight, like he would when offering him a treat. "Show Starlight. What thinks he?"

Reg looked over at Starlight. "He's not interested in pictures."

Starlight walked over to Reg and stood up on his hind legs to see what she was holding. Feeling silly, Reg turned the pictures on the screen toward him. Starlight sniffed the edges of the phone, then stopped and looked solemnly at the pictures on the screen. He cocked his head to the side and peered at it for a long time. Then he sat down and began to wash.

Reg laughed and turned the screen off. "That was funny."

"He knows humans do not have cat heads."

"Well… no, I guess he knows that."

"Humans have strange gods."

"Yeah. Some of them are," Reg agreed. She thought about the immortals and wondered how many times they had inspired the stories of the pantheons of gods. In school, they had talked about how the Romans had taken the Greek gods and renamed them, and in some cases merged more than one together or morphed details about them. But what if the Romans hadn't taken the Greek gods, but had just known the same immortals and called them by different names? And the gods in other cultures? The Norse and Egyptian pantheons? The Indian gods with multiple arms or blue skin? Had they all been inspired by Harrison, Weston, Destine, and the others? Had Bastet been a real woman? One who loved cats, like Harrison did?

Reg assumed they could take whatever form they liked. Maybe Bastet had made herself look like a woman with a cat's head. Or maybe she had taken the form of a cat. It wasn't out of the realm of possibility. Not after Reg had seen the Witch Doctor—Destine—

send his essence into the nine kattakyns. Maybe some of them natu-rally took the forms of cats. Or other animals that they had an affinity for.

"We ask a favor of the great Reg Rawlins," Ruan announced.

So they had gotten to the reason Calliopia and Ruan had really come. Not just to be friendly when they had seen that Reg's light was still on. And not to say a final farewell to her and Starlight.

CHAPTER TWENTY-THREE

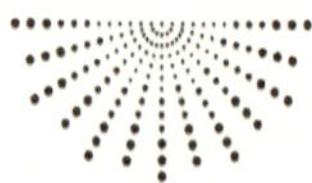

"What favor?" Reg asked with some reluctance. The two of them had divined gifts in Reg that she hadn't previously known that she had and, while that in itself wasn't necessarily a negative thing, she thought of the incident in the marina and wasn't so sure that she was ready to discover anything else new about herself. Especially not in front of witnesses.

Ruan bowed his head slightly in deference.

Calliopia grasped the cat pendant. "You will put power into the cat?" she ventured. "We travel far. We know not when we return. Perhaps we will need—I will need—its healing when I am far away."

Reg looked at the pendant. She wasn't sure what she was able to do with an inanimate object. She knew that she had pushed the heat from her inner fire into the pendant before, and that had seemed to help give Calliopia comfort and healing. But she didn't know how much she could put into it, and how long or far it would last. It would only be a temporary help to Calliopia. Something she could call on once or twice, and then it would be drained. She had strengthened Starlight and Calliopia directly, and supposed she could try to do that to the pendant, but she didn't have the same affinity for the object as Calliopia did. It had harmed both of them before the dagger had been unmade and formed into the cat. Reg had felt some of its magical pull when she carried it, but not to the extent that Calliopia had.

She glanced at Vivian, who was watching her with amusement. She supposed Vivian thought she was going to put on a show for the two 'children.' That she had duped them into believing that she had some kind of magical powers that she couldn't possibly have. Little did Vivian know the extent of what Reg had done in the past. And what she had nearly done.

Reg finally nodded. "Yes, okay. Do you want to take it off and give it to me?"

Calliopia looked at Reg with hooded eyes for a moment, suspicious about the request. She could leave it on if she wanted to. Reg could sit beside her and hold it while Callie wore it. Or she could try to do the magic from a distance. But it would be easier if she could just hold it in her hand. After a long period of consideration, Calliopia removed the pendant and handed it to Ruan, who handed it to Reg. Reg sensed Ruan's surprise rather than seeing a change in his expression. Reg doubted if Calliopia had removed the pendant since Reg had given it to her.

Reg felt the familiar warmth of the metal in her hand. As soon as it was in Reg's possession, she fought the desire to keep it for herself. It wanted her to own it. It wanted her to put it in her pocket or around her neck and to keep it for herself. It was warm and friendly and would protect her.

She forced her mind away from these paths. It was Calliopia's pendant. She would need it. She had needed it to heal and hopefully it would help with her continued recovery. Reg was just holding it to facilitate Calliopia's improved health and strength.

Calliopia was going away. She was going to need everything Reg could put into the pendant. She focused on it, squeezing it tightly in her hands. She forced heat into it until it was almost too hot to hold. Then she thought about the healing that Calliopia needed. Not just the dreadful knife wound in her side that was slowly knitting back together, but also her mind. The nightmares and dark visions that she saw. What Reg might consider PTSD if Calliopia were human. She was hypervigilant, always watching for the return of the shadows that had stolen her away once. There was no way for her to fight the demons that no one else could see, and trying to do so had resulted in the wound that had very nearly killed her.

Reg thought about all that Calliopia needed. She would be leaving her mother and father again, the two people—other than Ruan—who loved her most in the world. She would be removing herself from their love and comfort and they wouldn't be able to help her anymore. She was cut off from the rest of fairy society and could not return to it due to her choice of mate. She had chosen a pixie who naturally craved the damp, dark underground, while she sought the sun and the light, running from the shadows. She would need comfort and strength in her body and mind if she were going to get better.

She put all of that into the pendant. All that she could, anyway. After a few minutes, Starlight jumped up into her lap and nosed at the cat pendant, and Reg held it still and joined her strength with his to put everything she could into it. They wouldn't be back for her to refill it. Not in the near future, anyway. Whatever she could manage, that would be it.

When she couldn't squeeze any more healing thoughts into it, Reg again heated it, hoping to seal it in and to combine the health and heat into something that was more than the sum of the parts. When she couldn't do anything more, she handed it back to Calliopia, reaching across the coffee table. She bumped Vivian's arm as she did so and Vivian jerked back as if she'd been burned.

Calliopia took the pendant back and held it against her chest, looking like a woman who had thought she would never get her precious treasure back again. She nodded her thanks.

"Reg Rawlins is most gracious. Most powerful of humans," Ruan said.

Reg cleared her throat. "That might be a bit of an exaggeration," she said, flushing. But she had learned that Ruan tended to use formal, over-the-top language in his compliments. Calliopia, on the other hand, was more likely to be blunt in the manner of the fairies, seemingly not realizing the difference between a compliment and an insult.

Reg cleared her throat and glanced over at Vivian to roll her eyes and shrug it off. But Vivian was wide-eyed and acted as if she were afraid of something.

As someone who had faced runaway trucks and lions and house-crushing boulders in her life, Reg was surprised that she would be afraid of anything. Reg looked at Ruan and at the door and the window, looking for what it was that had disturbed Vivian. But nothing seemed to be out of place.

"It's getting late," Vivian said, catching Reg's eyes on her.

"It's not that bad. Calliopia and Ruan are leaving now, you and I can spend a bit more time together trying to sort this out."

Vivian shook her head. "No. I have to go."

She stood up, checked to make sure that she had her purse and touched her chest where her gold cat pendant was hidden. She hurried toward the door. Starlight made a dash for it and reached the door before Vivian.

"Wait! Don't let him out. Let me grab him!" Reg called out.

Vivian reached for the doorknob. Starlight danced up on his hind legs and batted at her, snagging a claw on her shirt. Reg had never seen him behave like that before.

"Starlight! Just wait for a minute, Vivian. I don't know why he's acting like this. Just give me a second to get him out of your way."

She hurried over and grabbed Starlight, who yowled in protest. Reg struggled to get his claw out of Vivian's blouse, and saw that it pulled a thread, puckering the fabric. She winced and hoped that Vivian wouldn't notice it.

But of course she would. She couldn't help seeing it.

"Sorry. I'm sorry. We'll talk later, okay? Call me."

Vivian wrenched open the door and marched out without another word.

Reg turned back to face Ruan and Calliopia. "Sorry about that… I'm not sure what she was so upset about. Or what's going on with Starlight. But… well… good luck on your journey. You'll… take care of each other."

Ruan nodded. "We will, Reg Rawlins. And you and Starlight take care of each other."

"Okay. We will. You guys will be okay?" Reg's eyes went to Calliopia. "Callie?"

Calliopia had put the necklace back on, and she held it at her throat. "We will be fine. Thank you, Reg Rawlins, for all."

"You're welcome. I'm glad… I could help."

Calliopia nodded. She looked down at the pendant, and then over at Starlight. "He is a powerful being."

Reg bit her lip. "I wish I knew more about him. I feel like everyone can see something in him that I can't."

"You know him better than others."

"I know I should… but I don't think I do."

CHAPTER TWENTY-FOUR

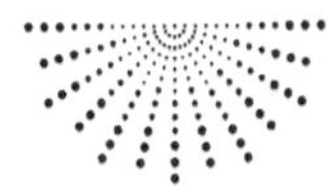

After everyone was gone, Reg wasn't sure what to do with herself. She looked down at Starlight.

"What was that about? Why did you go after Vivian like that?"

He sat back on his haunches, looking inscrutable. Reg put her hands on her hips. "Why is it that everyone knows more about you than I do? I know that you picked me, but I don't know why. Because you knew my father? Did you want to protect me or for me to do something for you? Or did you just want to be around someone familiar?"

He stood up and rubbed against her legs, not saying anything. Reg sighed. She picked him up and scratched his chin. "Did you pick me because you saw me when I was a little girl? Because I wanted you back then?"

He rubbed against her chin, purring. Reg got warm feelings from him, but not an impression as to why he had picked her. Maybe it was just as simple as that—he liked her, so he wanted to be with her.

"I suppose we should go to bed. After putting so much power into that pendant, I don't think I can manage much else. And I want to stay strong so that..." she trailed off, not wanting to say it out loud.

That she had to stay strong to fight any siren urges.

* * *

Reg and Damon had planned to meet each other in the afternoon after Damon finished acting as a security guard for a conference. Reg was glad for the opportunity. She needed to do something that was just pleasant and relaxing instead of worrying about Vivian and what kind of accident she was going to be in next. Or Reg's newly-discovered siren problem. They were going to get a bite to eat from one of the food trucks that set up near the conference center and go for a walk. Nice and relaxing. Nothing taxing, but also nothing too romantic. Reg liked Damon as a friend, but she still wasn't sure about him as a romantic prospect. Like Corvin, he was dark-haired, with short whiskers in a goatee. Handsome, though not bewitching like Corvin. Reg had never had the same chemistry with him as with Corvin. Not Damon's fault, of course.

Damon did have the gift of being able to put visions of his own construction into other people's heads. Something that Reg had warned him several times that she did not want him to do without permission. Damon had his difficulties in following this dictum. He said that it was just one of the ways that he communicated and Reg was putting an unfair restriction on their relationship. Reg didn't mind the visions so much; it wasn't like he'd put anything in her head that was disturbing or traumatizing. Usually, his visions were quite pleasant, designed to relax her or to encourage her to do something with him. Sort of like the trailers before a movie—a taste of how pleasant and enjoyable it would be to spend the time with him.

She just didn't like the fact that he could put it in her head without her permission. She wanted to be in control and to know where all of her thoughts and visions were coming from. His visions could be so realistic that sometimes she was left disoriented, feeling a step out of time because she thought something had happened when it hadn't.

But they were getting more used to each other. More comfortable and in tune with the other's quirks.

Reg was watching the time so that she wouldn't be late meeting him. She was a couple of minutes later than she had intended and looked along the sidewalk for him, worried that he'd be standing around waiting and might think that she had stood him up.

But she didn't see him. It would probably take him time to make sure that everyone had dispersed from the conference he had been supervising and to clock out or whatever else he had to do at the end of his shift. Maybe change into a fresh shirt.

So she sat back and relaxed, watching the people walking around her, happy to be on their lunch breaks. Looking at the different food trucks to try to decide what she would order. There were lots of options. Reg could smell onion rings and was reminded of her childhood. There had only been one fast-food joint in town that sold onion rings, and the rest of the foster kids she was with at the time didn't like onion rings, so the family never bought them when they made a rare excursion out for fast food. So the only way that Reg could get any was if she managed to get her hands on some money to pay for them. She would search for coins in the furniture or left out on dressers or in coat pockets. She would collect bottles and cans to take to the bottle depot for refund. Sometimes she would hang around the supermarket to help overburdened moms with their groceries, hoping for a few cents for tips. And when she had accumulated enough, she would get on one of the boys' bikes and pedal over to the Burger Stop to get an order of hot, crispy onion rings all for herself.

There was a knock on the window. Reg jumped, startled out of her memory, and saw Damon looking at her, eyebrows raised. She opened the door and climbed out of the car.

"Sorry," Damon apologized. "I didn't mean to scare you."

"Oh, it's okay, I was just daydreaming." She shut and locked her door. "How was work?"

"Good. Glad that one is over."

"Oh?"

"Some of these things just always end up being constant problems. And you can never predict which ones they will be."

"Yeah? What was this one?"

"Meteorologists."

"What?" Reg frowned. "What does a meteorologist do?" She had the idea that it must be something to do with space. Maybe like an astrologer? Looking to the skies to predict the future or divine something that had happened in the past?

Damon gave her a grin. "Weather people."

"Weather people? Like they control the weather?"

"Nope, just predict it."

Reg shook her head. "I've never heard of that." She thought she had heard about most of the magical gifts. But it seemed there was always one more that she hadn't heard of before.

"Sure you have." Damon laughed. "On the radio? The TV? Your weather app? People who predict the weather."

"You mean… like the regular weatherman?"

"Yes. The regular weatherman."

"Not a practitioner?"

"Well, I imagine there were probably one or two there incognito, but yes, just non-magical meteorologists. People who appear on your early-morning show to tell you how to prepare for the morning commute."

"Oh." Reg laughed at herself and shook her head. Her braids swung one way and then the other, making a comforting sound when they hit each other. "I didn't know that you did security for normal conferences too. I just assumed they were all for magical conferences and meetings."

"A lot of them are, but I still get run-of-the-mill everyday kinds of conferences too. And surprisingly enough, those are some of the most difficult ones."

"Really?"

"Really. You can never predict." He grinned. "Kind of like the weather."

"Ah." Reg laughed at his joke. "Don't let them hear you say that."

"Exactly. These people are very high-strung. I rarely have physical fights break out at my conferences, and this one had three!"

"Sheesh. They really are serious about their jobs, aren't they?"

"I know. It's weird, right? I don't usually have to deal with bad behavior from practitioners. The occasional small fire to put out," he winked at Reg, "but nothing I can't easily handle."

"Good thing."

"So…" Damon stretched his arms behind him to pop his shoulders. He rolled them, loosening up his muscles, showing her that he was ready to relax and enjoy her company. "Have you looked around to decide what you're going to get? There are a lot of good choices. I can tell you what the most popular places are. And some of the hidden jewels. I've eaten at most of them at one time or another."

Reg gestured toward the Burger Barn. "I can smell the onion rings at that one. I have to have them."

He raised his brows. "Sure. They're always popular."

Reg thought belatedly that he might not want her to have onion rings if they were going to be getting close to each other, talking, breathing in each other's faces… she hadn't even thought of the evils of onion breath.

"I might have to steal one or two of them from you," Damon said. "I can't get a full order—they give me terrible heartburn—but I could have a couple small ones, if I'm eating something else that's not deep-fried."

"Sure." Reg had liked the idea of having a full order to herself, just like when she used to go to the Burger Stop, but she wasn't going to begrudge him a couple of rings. Unless the order size was really skimpy. "So what else, do you think? Should I just stay with the Burger Barn and have… a burger? I assume that's their specialty."

"They're pretty good… but they're better known for their milkshakes. The best burgers are probably at Sneaky Pete's." Damon shrugged. "They've won awards."

"They must be good, then."

"Are you adventurous? There are a couple of trucks that sell more… unusual fare."

"Like what?" Reg was suspicious. In her mind, adventurous usually meant disgusting, and she wasn't going to ruin her lunch date by eating something gross.

"Well… some rare meats. Or the Creamery has all kinds of flavors of ice cream that you never even thought of. They have some flower-infused ones, like lavender or chamomile."

"Do they have chocolate?"

"They probably have twenty different kinds of chocolate."

"Then I'll go there for dessert. And I'll try the burgers at Sneaky Pete's."

"Sounds good. I think I'm going for the taco of the future."

"The taco of the future?" Reg repeated.

Damon pointed to a food truck with a rocket ship on top. "It might not exactly be traditional Mexican fare, but it's good. It is… the taco of the future."

"Okay… are we sure?"

A wrinkle appeared between Damon's eyebrows. "What?"

"I mean has someone actually traveled to the future to verify that? Or at least seen a vision of the future? I mean… they could get arrested for false advertising. It happens, you know."

Damon's expression relaxed into a smile. "You've got a point there. I'll have to ask them. I'm not aware of any certification of their taco of the future designation."

Reg nodded. "You have to make sure you're not getting scammed," she laughed.

Damon agreed. They split up to get their lunches, and then met up near Reg's car.

"We could try to get a table," Damon said, looking around at the picnic tables under the trees in the nearby park. "Or a patch of grass. Or eat and walk while we talk."

"My foster mom Carrie always said that if you walked while you ate, you'd get gas and wouldn't digest your food properly," Reg offered.

"Okay. So you want to sit? Tables or grass?"

"No. Let's walk and eat."

He chuckled. "I should have known as much. Have you ever been known to actually take anyone's advice?"

"A foster mom's? Probably not. Maybe someone who didn't have an agenda. Or someone who said not to get too close to the lion's cage at the zoo. But parents and teachers…?" Reg sighed. "I was a little… stubborn."

At Damon's skeptical look, she rolled her eyes.

"Okay, maybe a lot stubborn."

CHAPTER TWENTY-FIVE

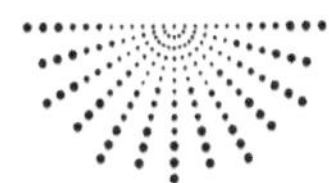

They started down the sidewalk that led to the pathways through the park. Reg's comment about the lion at the zoo brought Vivian to mind and, as they walked and ate, she related some of the story to Damon. She tried not to share anything private about her clients, but the stuff that was well-known, especially the things that had been on TV, she could tell him.

"Wow, she's got a serious case of bad luck." Damon wiped a red smear of taco sauce off of his cheek and licked his fingers. His taco of the future, soon to become a taco of the past, was dripping everywhere.

"Yes," Reg agreed. "I've tried to get some more information from her to figure out why... but so far... not much luck. It's been since she was a little girl, so her memories aren't really clear."

"Maybe even something her parents did. She might not even have been in the room, if they offended some magical being who decided to take out his anger on their progeny... which would also explain them deciding not to have any other children."

"Do you think so?" Reg thought about it. She didn't know much about the types of curses that could cause a situation like the one Vivian was in. "That's not really fair... to punish her for something that her parents did."

"A lot of magical beings wouldn't give a darn. And others believe in retribution on all the generations to come. You anger one of them, and your family might be dealing with the pox until the entire line has finally died out."

"Yikes. What kind of beings would do that?"

"Ogres. Cyclopes. Immortals. I don't know. Some of the ancient races are really into that kind of thing. You'd think we were still stuck in pre-Roman eras." Damon stuffed the last of his taco in his mouth, then proceeded to lick off all of his fingers before wiping them with a soggy napkin, making her think of Starlight washing himself after eating. She smiled and kept this tidbit to herself.

"Well, I don't know if it could be something like that. Vivian didn't say anything to indicate that it was a family thing… but like you said, she might not even know."

"I would think, though, that she would have some idea from the things that might have happened to her parents. If they died sudden, gruesome deaths…"

"I don't think so. Not that she ever said. The only thing that I remember her saying about her parents… She said that they had done well with their archaeology finds. She said that they were quite 'comfortable.'"

Damon took one of Reg's onion rings. She had only eaten half of them so far, and a few bites of the enormous Barn Burger she had ordered. She'd had no idea that it would actually be as big as a barn. She didn't object to Damon taking one of the onion rings. She was going to have to either get him to eat part of the burger as well, or she was going to have to toss it in the garbage. Having gone through some very lean times, she hated to throw food away. But she needed to save room for chocolate ice cream…

She'd looked into the Creamery truck as she'd walked by. She didn't think they had twenty different flavors of chocolate ice cream; they wouldn't be able to fit that many into one truck. But even so, she saw several varieties of chocolate, and was thinking about one that had appeared to have globs of fudgy chocolate and caramel swirls.

"Well, that could point to a broken covenant," Damon suggested. "Maybe they had promised something to a magical being, maybe a guardian of some sort of treasure, and then they ended up breaking their covenant. So a curse has been set on their descendants as a consequence."

"Yeah. Could be. That might make sense."

Damon put his arm around Reg's waist as they walked. She was still eating, so holding hands was out of the question, but she wasn't sure about the contact. They were friends, but they hadn't really advanced to the boyfriend-girlfriend zone. She shifted away from him, and he let his hand fall back to his side. He hooked his thumbs into his pockets casually and said nothing about it.

"She sounds like an exciting client."

"Mmm-hmm," Reg agreed around a large bite of Barn Burger. She chewed and swallowed. "But I'm not sure that an exciting client is what I want. Jacky was pretty exciting, and I'm still recovering from that one."

"Yes," Damon agreed, nodding vigorously. "We don't need any more like her around."

They had both suffered harm at Jacky's hand. Reg shook her head, thinking about it. "How are you doing? Are you fully recovered?"

"I feel fine. They still want me to go back for tests every few months, until they've decided that there's no lasting organ damage. You?"

"Yeah, but I'm not going to bother, I don't think. I'm okay, and I don't feel like paying for all of those visits and tests."

Damon nodded. "It's not cheap. But..." He looked at her sideways. "You can afford it now, can't you?"

Reg didn't answer. One of the problems with Damon was that he was a diviner, a human lie detector, and Reg was... someone with a lot of practice telling lies. She was used to people not being able to tell when she was lying about something, but Damon was different. He said he didn't expect people to tell the truth all of the time, but Reg got self-conscious around him, knowing that he was always listening to what she said for the ring of truth.

"What makes you say that?" she asked after a long, silent pause.

"I just thought... it seems like you've been more comfortable lately. Financially speaking. I gathered that you have come into some money."

Reg bit her lip.

She still hadn't told Damon or any of the others who had been on her quest to the Blue Ridge Mountains that she had been compensated by Calliopia's parents, the Papillons. They had been very grateful for everything Reg had done for Calliopia when everyone else had thought that there was no hope for her survival. It was Reg who had seen to it that she was healed. And they had sent her a personal gift that had been rather generous. And maybe she should have shared it with her friends.

Damon made a careless gesture with one hand. "Doesn't make any difference," he said. "Just observing."

Reg still didn't answer. It was too awkward. She looked for a change of subject.

"What other conferences do you have coming up? Anything else as exciting as a meeting of weathermen?"

"Some of them are women," Damon said. "We can't forget them."

"No. No, I didn't mean to be sexist about it. In fact, I'll bet that most of the fights were between the women."

"You wouldn't be wrong."

Reg couldn't say she was surprised. Some of the most vicious fighters she'd seen had been girls, not boys. The boys at least seemed to have some sense of fair play and unwritten rules. The girls didn't have the same scruples.

"So? Anything good coming up?"

"I don't think so. We've got Spring Games coming up, but not for a little while yet."

"What is the Spring Games?"

"Sort of like the Olympics of the magical world. A big do the week of equinox."

"That sounds interesting. I'll bet they need a lot of security at something like that."

"They do. They'll have a lot of out of town talent as well. Since I'm local and the games are being held here, I'll be in the 'upper management.' It's a good contract; I'll make a good bit of coin at that one."

"Great. Good for you. You must be happy about that."

"It hasn't even started yet, but I'll be glad when it's over. I know it's going to be chaotic and exhausting. Worth it, but I wish I could skip over all of the middle parts."

Reg nodded. "Yeah, I get that. I wouldn't mind going straight for the money, and not having to do anything in between."

CHAPTER TWENTY-SIX

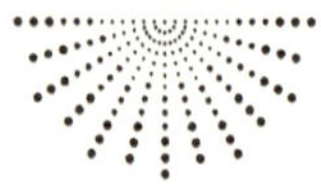

s they looped around and began to walk back toward the starting point, Reg disposed of what was left of her burger. She was starting to feel too full already and she wanted that ice cream.

The crowds were thinning out, most of the regular workers having to return to their jobs in the afternoon. Reg hadn't thought about what time the food trucks would start packing up. She looked at her phone. "Are they all going to be closing? I still wanted to get some ice cream."

"The Creamery will probably stick around for a bit longer. The trucks that are just main courses will be mostly gone by the time we get back there."

"Let's hurry. I don't want to miss it."

Damon smiled and picked up his pace a little. They weren't running, but they were no longer strolling along without a care either. Reg wanted her fudgy caramel swirl ice cream.

They were almost back to the street the food trucks were parked on when there was a loud boom, like a truck had lost its load or gone over train tracks. She looked in the direction she thought the noise had come from and saw a black billow of smoke. She blinked, thinking at first that she was just imagining things. Then she clutched Damon's arm. "Do you see that? Was that…?"

He had been looking the other direction, watching a dog that was tearing around the park loose, with no leash on and no obvious owner nearby to keep him under control. He turned around with a smile, opening his mouth to say something to Reg. He followed her gaze and the blood left his face.

"That's the conference center. I need to… I need to go!" He seemed to be trapped between running over to see what had happened and saying a proper goodbye to Reg.

She pushed him away. "Go!"

He looked grateful and took off at a run.

People were already starting to gather, staring at the smoke coming out of the building, the first of the observers beginning to pull out their phones to video the scene. Reg swallowed, watching it. What had happened? She hoped that it was just a blown A/C unit or something that could be easily replaced and hadn't actually done any damage to the building.

But she knew it wasn't the case.

The black smoke billowing out a couple of the windows of the building was too much to be something that was small and unimportant.

Sirens started in the distance. Reg wondered how large the Black Sands fire department was. It was a small town. Probably a volunteer fire department. A few trucks. Would it be enough to put out the fire?

Forgetting about the ice cream, Reg walked toward the building. Unlike Damon, she didn't belong there. The building and the occupants were not her responsibility. Even though Damon was off the clock, it was part of his job to make sure that people at the conference center stayed safe some of the time. He knew the building and the staff and probably knew all of the emergency evacuation procedures.

But Reg hadn't even been inside. The tribunal she had gone to had been in one of the hotels, not the conference center. She had no idea of the layout and didn't know anything about what to do in case of fire. Other than what she had learned about in school. Stop, drop, and roll. Stay low. Break a window. She had lived in a couple of foster homes with firebugs, and they had done fire drills and repeated the safety instructions repeatedly. But getting herself out of a burning house and helping when something like the conference center was on fire were two very different things.

She couldn't help being drawn toward the building. It wasn't until she was close, and the fire engines drawing up behind her, that she stopped to think about her firecasting gift. She had a gift for starting fires and feeding the flames. Not so much for putting them out. If she got too close, it was possible that she wouldn't be able to stop herself from feeding the flames. *Playing with fire,* Davyn her mentor would call it with a fond smile. But he wouldn't be smiling if she sent a public building up in an inferno. She stopped in her tracks and swore.

What was she to do? She didn't want to be one of the observers. One of the people standing around tweeting and live casting the fire. She wanted to help.

People were coming out of the building in a steady stream. It had only been a couple of minutes since the explosion. The building was being evacuated. Reg knew she couldn't go inside. Not only because she might make the fire worse, but because everyone would know you weren't supposed to walk back into a burning building, and would stop her. The firefighters behind her would be cordoning off the area and keeping anybody from going inside. It was their job to go in with their equipment and to search for any stragglers, anyone trapped inside.

"Reg?"

Reg looked around at the sound of her name. It was a female voice, not Damon's. Damon was nowhere in sight. Had he gone into the building? She hated to think that he could get trapped inside there. Even just the smoke could kill him, to say nothing of the flames or any collapsing structure. She should have stopped him, but instead, she had told him to go.

Her eyes caught on a woman, but in the confusion, it was a few seconds before the woman's face and identity registered with Reg. She was too worried about Damon, the fire, and what was going to happen to the people left inside.

"Vivian?"

Vivian walked toward her, away from the building. A man caught her by the arm, jerking her to a stop. "Hey! You need to stay with your group. We have to account for everyone who was in the building. You need to wait here so we can be sure that everyone gets out."

Vivian pulled her arm away from him. "I'm not going anywhere," she snapped. But despite her words, she took a couple of steps toward Reg. "Reg, what are you doing here?"

"I was just… lunch…" Reg couldn't form a full thought. "What are you…?"

"I was just signing up for a course. They have one on dealing with insurance claims, and I thought that it would be good…" She trailed off.

Reg was surprised that with Vivian's history of accidents that she would need any help navigating an insurance claim. But hadn't she said she couldn't get insurance?

"You were in there?" she asked. "What happened? Do you know?"

Vivian shook her head. Her eyes were dark and hooded. Damon would know whether she was telling the truth, but Reg strongly suspected that she was not. "I don't know… there was just a noise, and then all of the smoke. Someone pulled the fire alarm, or maybe it went off automatically because of the smoke, and then everybody was trying to get out…" She looked back at the people still coming out of the building. "Everyone was pushing and shouting, and we couldn't use the elevators. The emergency lights didn't come on in the stairways, so everyone was using their phone lights to see and find their way out." She shook her head. "The smoke was getting so thick, so fast…" She coughed.

"Was everyone okay? Did everyone get out?" Reg knew that Vivian wasn't in charge of the evacuation and that people were still coming out behind her, but the words just came out. She needed reassurance.

"I guess. I didn't see anyone trapped. People were pushing, but they weren't getting trampled."

Reg shuddered. She wished that Vivian hadn't gone into that building. If she had just stayed away, it would have been fine. Why was fate so determined to exterminate her?

"You're okay?" Reg asked, more calmly. Vivian had left their last meeting abruptly and, if Reg were going to find out anything more about her strange curse, she needed to approach the matter delicately, not to trigger whatever it was that had upset Vivian before.

"I'm fine." Vivian looked back at the building. "I'm just fine," she repeated.

"Do you think…" Reg didn't know quite how to put her question into words in a tactful way. "You don't think that this was because of…"

Vivian shook her head adamantly and looked around, not wanting anyone to hear Reg making any accusations. She took another step toward Reg, but the man who clearly took his position as a fire marshal very seriously again grabbed her by the arm, and he pulled her violently back.

"I told you, you need to stay here with everyone else. No one is to leave the muster points."

The firefighters were pulling hoses off of the trucks and barking at people to move out of the way. There were a few policemen and security guards around, but the fire department appeared to have beaten most of the police department there. Reg moved to the side and tried to stay out of their way. She tried to keep Vivian in sight. She didn't want something to happen to her client before they had a chance to talk again.

Reg looked toward the building, hoping to see Damon. She could hear creaking and crackling noises coming from inside the building, and there was a pressure building inside her chest. The fire was growing, consuming everything it could, growing exponentially like a monster that would soon devour the entire building and anything else left within it.

Even the firemen started to shield their faces and stood back, watching and waiting. The stream of people exiting the building had slowed to a trickle and then stopped. Reg still didn't see Damon anywhere. She scanned the crowds. There were too many people for her to be sure. He wasn't wearing his black warlock robes, but navy pants and a white shirt, blending in with the many other businessmen who had exited the building. She was sure he was there; she just couldn't see him yet.

Reg could no longer hear the shouts of the firemen around her. She knew they were conversing back and forth, both over their radios and by shouting to each other, but they seemed like they were far away from her. Like there was a barrier between them.

She tried to suppress the fire. When the fire inside her flared out of control, Davyn had her calm it and squeeze it smaller.

There was so much of it, spread over several floors, still looking for more fuel. Most of the oxygen had been sucked out of the building. Windows shattered as the heat intensified. Reg closed her eyes and tried harder. She had power. She had plenty of power if she concentrated and stayed focused.

She drew more energy from the people around her. They weren't aware of what she was doing, yet they grew quieter, perhaps sensing that something had changed. Maybe feeling some of the power draining out of them. Instead of the adrenaline rush they had been experiencing, they were losing momentum. They stopped talking and yelling so much, made space for the firefighters, and turned their eyes away from their phones and to each other. Reg tried to smother the fires. She sensed that there were multiple fires; it wasn't just one inferno anymore. She squashed the smaller ones and tried to make a wall around the big ones, to contain them until the firefighters could do something.

CHAPTER TWENTY-SEVEN

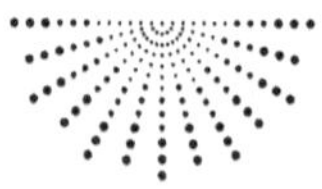

Then suddenly, Reg was inside the building. The smoke was so thick she couldn't see and couldn't breathe. Her lungs burned. The heat inside the building, even where there were no flames, was enough to cook her flesh. She tried to make peace with the fire, to use her affinity to stop it from burning her, but it didn't work.

"Ma'am, you need to move back!"

Someone shoved Reg back, and she was pulled out of the vision. She breathed clean, oxygenated air and looked around. If it was a vision, had she seen it because she was trying to dampen the fire, or was there another reason?

Damon.

Reg looked for him again in the crowds outside the building. There was no sign of him. Reg grabbed one of the firemen. "My friend is in there."

"The building has been evacuated, ma'am. She'll be around here somewhere."

"No, he went in to help. He's a security guard. He went in, and he hasn't come back out."

"He could be on the other side of the building. You don't know."

Reg tried to see the vision again, to get some detail of where

Damon was. She was able to connect to him again quickly. She felt dizzy and faint. The fumes of burning synthetics choked her. "He's there… with other people. He was helping to clear bathrooms. There was a woman with children…"

The firefighter stared at her through the face shield. "What are you talking about?"

"I can see him. I see where he is. It's the main floor. There are accessible toilets. They aren't in the same place as the main women's and men's bathrooms. You need to go there and get them out."

"You don't know that. I have a job to do. Let me do it."

"I do know." Reg held on to him as tightly as she could, knowing that he was going to pull away and shake her off. "I can see them!"

"Ma'am."

"Please!" She tried to project the image to him. Somehow, she needed to make him understand. He was a resident of Black Sands. He had to have seen some pretty weird stuff in the past. Even if he didn't really believe in magic, he had to know from living there that some things couldn't be explained. "You have to get him and that family out."

He hesitated for a minute. Then he pulled away. "Main floor accessible toilet."

"Yes. Please."

He nodded. He hurried away from her, toward the burning building, talking into his radio. Telling them to help him to get to the restroom? Or to keep the crazies back out of the way so he could get his job done?

That was all Reg could do. She couldn't go in there herself. She didn't have any equipment or training. All she could do was wait outside.

And do what she could to calm the fire.

She leaned against a tree, her knees shaking like jelly, and again began to pull strength from the crowd surrounding the building. She pictured the area where Damon and the others were trapped and concentrated her efforts there. Putting out the smaller fires and trapping the bigger ones behind walls. Trying to create an invisible barrier between the little family and Damon, and the flames. Damon crawled over to the sink and began running the water. He soaked handfuls of paper towels and he and the woman tried to hold them over their own faces and the children's.

Reg sank to the ground. How long would it take the firefighters to get to them? Had the man believed her? Were they trying to get in and clear a safe path to retrieve them?

The seconds ticking away seemed like hours and days. Reg pressed her palms to her eyes, trying to keep her focus.

Finally, she heard the shouting and the rushing of the water hoses. The crashing as they pushed in through the door and looked for the survivors. Reg's throat swelled so that she could hardly breathe or swallow the lump, impossibly grateful that the firemen had reached Damon and the family.

Between them, the firefighters managed to help the children and mother out the door, shielding them from the flames. Damon stuck close to them, struggling for breath but managing to get out under his own power. Reg waited until they were all out of the building before letting go.

CHAPTER TWENTY-EIGHT

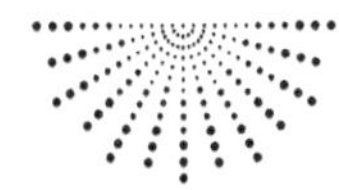

"Reg? Reg, are you okay?"

Reg didn't want anyone to touch her. She kept her eyes closed, batting away at the hands that interfered with her sleep. She needed to rest. For just a few more minutes. She didn't want to go to school yet.

"Reg. Wake up. Reg!"

The insistent voice wouldn't go away. Reg tried to pry her eyes open. She blinked blearily, looking around, not sure what was going on. There were a lot of people around. She was napping underneath a tree. There seemed to be a lot of excitement. Davyn was crouched down next to her.

"Hey. Hi, Davyn."

"Are you alright? What happened?" Davyn looked over his shoulder toward the conference center, but it was blocked by the crowds watching it. There was smoke coiling into the sky. "Reg, tell me that you didn't…"

"What?" Reg sat up, blinking her eyes and trying to sort out her fuzzy brain. "What's going on?"

"There's a fire. Did you have something to do with this?"

A fire. Reg tried to remember all that had happened. She felt weak. Like she had just run a marathon. Not that she had ever run a marathon.

"No. Why would you think that?"

"I don't want to think that you could have. I told you not to experiment, not to practice any firecasting without me."

"I didn't."

"How did this start, then?"

"It wasn't anything to do with me." Reg rubbed her eyes. They stung from the smoke. Her head was thick and it was difficult to breathe through her stuffed-up nose. "I don't know what happened. Maybe a bomb. I was walking in the park." She looked in the direction of the food trucks. "And there was a boom and then smoke started to pour out."

It started to come back to her. More details of why she had been there and what had happened.

"Where's Damon? Is he okay?"

"I'm sure he's fine. Tell me what happened next. Why are you so tired?"

"Damon was in the building. You have to make sure he's okay."

"He was in the building when the fire started?"

"No. He went in to help. And he got trapped. There were people in there, he was helping to get them out, and he got trapped in the bathroom. I told the firefighters." Reg rubbed her head. She had a headache. A really bad one. Like when she was a kid and got badly dehydrated at school track and field day and threw up. "I told them, and I tried to quiet the fire. Tried to keep Damon and the others from getting hurt until they could get them out."

Davyn raised his brows, eyes widening. "You did that?" He looked toward the conference center. "From out here? That would take a huge amount of energy. It looks like it was a massive fire."

Reg nodded. "It was. Really big. I took energy from the other people."

"The other people?"

Reg motioned to the crowd. "The bystanders. Everyone was standing around, all excited, so I... borrowed some of their energy."

"Borrowed?" Davyn repeated, his lip curling.

"Well… I guess technically, I'm not going to be giving it back, so maybe it wasn't exactly borrowing, but they would have given it to me if they had known. They wanted to help."

"Oh, I see. And you could tell that they wouldn't be upset if you skimmed their energy to help fight the fire."

"Well, they wouldn't, would they? Who would be upset about that? You'd help, if you could, wouldn't you? You'd want me to save Damon and the kids who were stuck in there."

Davyn rolled his eyes. "Yes, you know that I would, but that's not the same as asking permission. You're just taking. That's really frowned upon in magical society."

"I needed it to save Damon. You think I should just have let him die? Or should I have gone in there myself and gotten burned up too?"

"I didn't say that, Reg. But you have to think about what's ethical. You can't just take energy from people. How is that any different than Corvin taking your gifts away without you understanding what you were consenting to?"

"It is different." Reg scowled. "It was very different. No one's life was in danger. And he never planned to give them back, and I couldn't get them back any other way. These people just need to rest a little and have a hot dog, and they'll feel just fine. They'll get their energy back and not ever miss it. They'll think they just got overexcited or dehydrated out in the sun. It didn't hurt them."

"You can't know that. You can't know that there isn't someone here who might have chronic fatigue or some other medical condition, and taking their energy might have far-reaching consequences."

Reg shook her head. "Okay. Whatever." She rubbed her forehead. "Do you think you could get me… something to drink? I'm not feeling very good."

"Yes, of course." Davyn stood up and looked around. "I'll just be a minute. Stay here."

Reg closed his eyes again as he walked away. Where else was she going to go? She felt like death warmed over. Or death burned to a crisp. She was definitely feeling crispy.

Davyn returned a few minutes later with a water bottle and cracked it open for Reg.

"Here you go. How close did you get to the fire?"

"In real life? Not much closer than this. Just a few steps."

"In real life?" Davyn repeated.

"Yeah. But when Damon sent me a vision from inside, it was like I was inside with him, I could feel the heat and everything. So my body didn't actually go into the building, but it sure felt like I was there."

"And trying to tamp down on all of the flames inside… you're probably pretty dehydrated. Handling fire, you always need to be aware of your hydration level. It's easy to lose a lot of water without realizing what's going on."

Reg nodded. "Yeah. Feels like I've been out running in the sun all afternoon." She sipped the water slowly. She knew that guzzling it too fast, even if she were dangerously dehydrated, would result in her throwing it all back up, which wasn't helpful or pleasant.

Davyn sat down on the grass beside her.

"Did you see Damon?" Reg asked.

"Oh—yes, actually. I snagged the water bottle from one of the firefighter coolers, and Damon and some of the others who had smoke inhalation were over by the ambulance." Davyn gestured vaguely toward the emergency vehicles. "He looks okay, so don't worry. You got him out of there and he'll be just fine."

"And the woman and her kids? Are they okay too? I was so worried about them all."

Davyn nodded. "Yes, everyone looks okay. She had an older child with a wheelchair who she was changing at the time the room started to fill with smoke. She couldn't see well enough to get him back into his chair and he was too big for her to carry him out of there. So…" Davyn gave a broad shrug. "She needed help and it was a good thing that Damon was there, only he didn't manage to get out before things got too hot either."

"Literally," Reg quipped, and took another sip of the water.

"Literally," Davyn agreed. "Literally, too hot for them to get out of there without the firefighters to clear the way."

"Was anyone…" Reg looked toward the building, reaching out her psychic feelings, as much as she was able, to discover what she could feel. "Did everyone get out okay? They don't think that there's still anyone left inside? No one unaccounted for?"

"No. I don't think so. There's no sense of… panic or concern around the emergency vehicles. I don't think anyone is concerned about there being anyone inside."

"Good." Reg rested, waiting for her energy to start coming back. "I don't feel anyone."

"Just relax here for a while. I'm sure Damon will want to thank you once they let him go."

CHAPTER TWENTY-NINE

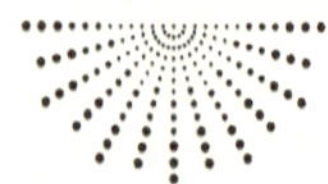

Vivian wanted to talk to Reg too. Not to thank her, maybe, but she wanted to have a word with Reg, and not in front of the two men she didn't know. She hung around, waiting for the others to disperse so that she could have a word with Reg alone, but Davyn and Damon weren't about to leave her side anytime soon.

"I'm sorry," Damon apologized, "I didn't mean to cause you any trouble… but I couldn't think of any other way to let anyone know that there were still people inside. I didn't even think I'd be able to reach you when we weren't in the same room. I haven't been able to cast a vision that far before."

"Maybe it was desperation," Davyn suggested. "You had a lot more motivation to get her the message than you normally would have. I hear that when soldiers start practicing with live grenades instead of duds, they can throw them twice as far."

"Motivation," Damon agreed, smiling. "Well, I certainly had that!"

He looked sunburned. His eyes were very red and swollen, and he was still coughing occasionally, a paramedic watching him from a distance away, not liking the fact that he wouldn't agree to be kept under observation at the hospital for the rest of the day. Reg remembered the heat of the fire, and worse, the acrid smoke that had burned all the way into her lungs and made her eyes stream with tears. She'd hardly been able to keep them open, the smoke stung so much.

"Are you sure you shouldn't go to the hospital for a while? Just to make sure you're okay?"

"I'm not going to the hospital." Damon coughed into his fist. "I'm just fine. A little irritation, that's all."

"I think it's more than that."

Damon eyed her but didn't argue. He knew that she was psychic. She could sense much of what he was feeling. And it would be a lie for him to tell her that he wasn't suffering more than he would like to admit.

"Maybe we should both go home," Reg offered. "Do you want to come over? We could keep an eye on each other."

Vivian was still hovering within earshot, and she looked irritated by the offer. She clearly had been hoping to get Reg's attention herself.

But Damon's health was more important. Vivian might be the one who kept narrowly escaping death, but she was escaping it and, as her parents had, Reg could only assume that she would continue to come out of the dreadful accidents unharmed. Damon might not be so lucky. And if it were Vivian's fault that the building had blown up to begin with…

Maybe Reg didn't want Vivian hanging around her house too much. She didn't want to make her own home a target for something disastrous to happen.

"I don't think either one of you is well enough to drive," Davyn pointed out.

Reg looked at Damon. She was okay to drive. But he was looking pretty grim. With his bloodshot eyes and lingering cough, he might be too distracted or unwell to drive.

"You are looking pretty tired," Damon agreed, looking back at Reg.

"I'm just tired, though. A few minutes sitting here, and I'll be just fine."

Davyn shook his head. "I don't want either of you driving. I'll give you a ride home. Especially if you're both going to go to Reg's. You can pick up your cars tomorrow."

"They'll get ticketed or towed."

"Then you pay it and appeal it after. It isn't like you don't have good reason for leaving your vehicles here overnight. No one can argue that you didn't have reason."

"Damon maybe," Reg said. "He can say that he was injured when he played hero. I can't exactly go to court and testify that I was too tired because I was psychically holding back the fire."

"Well, you could," Damon teased. "But they probably wouldn't believe you."

"Why don't you just shut up?" Reg returned good-naturedly.

* * *

In the end, they both let Davyn talk them into it. While they were both pretending to be feeling better than they actually were, neither could really deny it for long.

Reg fell asleep in the car on the way back to her house. Damon was looking pretty uncomfortable when they got out of the car.

"What is it?" Reg asked.

"I'm just wondering if maybe I could get a Tylenol."

"Yeah. Are those burns bad?"

"I'm not burned. Just… a little warm."

"You're burned."

The two of them shuffled down the pathway toward the cottage. "Why don't you let me heal you? I can do a little bit…"

"You're already drained. Just a Tylenol. I'll be fine."

"Or I could help," Davyn offered. "I haven't just been trying to put out a raging inferno with my powers. They are still intact."

"You should help Reg," Damon suggested. "You could give her a little bit more energy, couldn't you? Help her to recover faster?"

"I could do both, I suppose."

Reg let them into her cottage. It still caused her a little anxiety to allow any warlocks over her threshold, but neither of them had ever harmed or threatened her. Unlike Corvin, they were not likely to in the future. But she was still a little nervous whenever she let someone into her home. The wards were there to protect her against anyone with harmful intentions, but there were ways to bypass the wards.

She looked around the cottage. Nothing happened. She thought about how Sarah had showed her to detect whether there was a magic spell on the cookie, and to look around her kitchen and house with eyes that could see the spells and protections that had been placed there. She tried to do the same with her own home. It wasn't just familiar walls and furnishings. There was much more to it than that. Sarah had gone to considerable trouble to make sure it was a place that would be welcoming to Reg and her clients, and would keep her safe from harm.

What about Vivian? If she invited Vivian in yet again, would the protections that Sarah had set up on her own house and Reg's keep her safe? Or would Vivian's bad luck overpower everything else?

Looking around with new eyes, Reg could see the bright aura around several everyday items throughout the house. Around her doorknob and over the top of the doorway. Her stove. The hearth, as Sarah had called hers. In the living room area, Reg had left the crystal ball out on the coffee table, and there was a strong glow around it. Reg glanced around for more magical objects.

Starlight heard the door and company and left the bedroom where he was sleeping or watching out the window to meow at her and demand to be fed. Reg blinked her eyes as he walked toward her. His light was dazzling. The star between his eyes was like a headlight. Reg turned away and took a few breaths, consciously releasing her magical vision. When she looked back at Starlight, he looked just as he usually did. Just a regular black and white tuxedo cat. Her friend. The same one who cuddled up with her in the night when she was having nightmares.

It was no wonder, given how bright he had appeared to her, that other magical races commented on how powerful he was. How could his magic be that strong, and yet he still looked and acted just like a regular cat? And how had Norma Jean been able to cast such a strong spell over him?

"Everything okay, Reg?" Davyn asked. "Do you want me to give you an energy boost first?"

"No." Reg switched her attention back to her guests. "Do what you can for Damon first. He's in pain. I'm just tired. I can manage. Go to sleep if I have to."

"It's not that bad," Damon objected.

"Do him first," Reg repeated.

Davyn nodded, and he motioned for Damon to sit down on the wicker furniture. The two of them talked as Reg went to the fridge to find something for Starlight to eat, and shredded the meat from some leftover ribs into a bowl.

When she looked back at them, Damon seemed more at ease. More like himself. And his skin wasn't quite so red.

"That's better," Reg observed.

Damon nodded. "I told you it wasn't bad, just a little bit… warm."

"Scorched."

"Not scorched. Scorched is black. I just felt a little… flushed. Hardly anything."

Reg knew better. But she let it go. Let Damon have his ego. She looked over at Davyn. "And his lungs? Did you…"

"Yes," Davyn agreed. "I think he's going to be okay."

"Good. We'll hang out for the rest of the day. Then… he'll be fine tomorrow."

She didn't know whether she ought to make some kind of clarification about sleeping arrangements. She would send Damon home before she went to sleep. Or else Damon would sleep on the prickly wicker couch. Reg wasn't inviting him into her bed.

But she worried that trying to explain this would just result in Damon having hurt feelings and Davyn thinking that she was protesting too much and must therefore be covering up her true feelings. So she let it go. Davyn could think what he liked. Reg didn't owe him any explanation.

But she was uncomfortable with him thinking that she was pursuing relationships with both Corvin and Damon at the same time.

Which was not what she was doing.

Not at all.

* * *

When Davyn had finished, Damon had conked out on the couch. Davyn shook his head in amusement.

"I don't know if you'll be able to get him out of here tonight. Sleep is probably the best thing for him right now, while the body does its thing and continues to work on the healing process. But that means that you're not going to have the use of your couch for a while, and you'll have to put up with having a guest around."

"It's okay. I think I'm probably just going to go straight to bed anyway. In the morning, we can sort things out and he can head home. I'm sure he'll be feeling a lot better by then."

"I'm sure he will," Davyn agreed. "Now you remember… I don't want you practicing any firecasting while I'm not here."

"I can still put heat into him, help him to feel better that way."

"Yes… you can still do that, as long as you don't kindle fire. But you probably don't need to. Your energy is going to be at a premium for the next few days. I don't think you want to use it up on healing someone else. He's a tough guy. And I've done quite a bit for him."

Reg didn't make a comment one way or the other. "Well… thank you for looking after both of us today. I guess you probably didn't figure on that. It was nice of you to take the time, and to drive us here, do the healing, all of that. Above and beyond."

"Not at all. Happy to help out a couple of… members of my community."

Reg nodded. "Okay. I'm going to hit the sack, so we'll talk tomorrow."

Davyn took the hint and made his way to the door.

Reg was feeling quite a bit better. Not completely up to par, but he had given her enough strength that she could at least walk around the house without feeling like she needed a forklift to get her from one place to the other.

She stood there after Davyn was gone, looking at Damon snoring in her living room. She didn't really want to go straight to bed. Damon was taken care of for the night, but she knew that if she lay down to go to sleep, she would just end up tossing and turning, unable to get any sleep until the early hours of the morning. Better to do other things until her body was ready for sleep.

She grabbed a small tub of ice cream out of the freezer. It wasn't the fudgy chocolate and caramel swirl that she had been planning on before the fire had broken out, but it would have to do. She took it with her to the bedroom and lay down on the bed. She put her phone in front of her and checked out her latest video subscriptions. Starlight followed her into the bedroom and watched her, head cocked to the side at her strange behavior.

"I know, I know, no ice cream in the bedroom," Reg told him. "But I'm going to have to break the rule tonight. I can't exactly sit in the living room."

Of course, she could eat it at her kitchen table, which she never actually used, or she could sit in one of the chairs in the living room, but sitting there watching Damon sleep seemed a little creepy. She wanted to relax, and that meant lying down in the bedroom. All of the foster moms who had told her no food in the bedroom were just going to have to deal with it.

Reg tapped through the videos on her phone. There was one in the sponsored videos sidebar that was about discoveries in Egyptian tombs. Reg frowned. She supposed it was because she had previously searched for information on Bastet. That was why the app was offering something so different from what she usually watched.

CHAPTER THIRTY

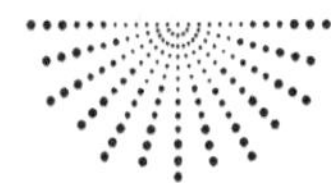

Reg didn't usually get up until late morning, or later, so it was a bit of a shock to her system to have someone wandering around her house earlier in the day, making coffee and trying to be quiet. But not really being quiet, because he probably wanted to talk to her about the previous day, or at least to say goodbye before he took off.

At first Reg had thought that it was Harrison. He was, after all, the only male human, or male-human-appearing being who was sometimes around her house while she was sleeping. After a few minutes of listening to Damon tip-toeing around her house, however, Reg had remembered enough of the previous day to put all of the details into place. She dragged herself out of bed, ran her fingers through her braids, and pulled on a housecoat that she rarely ever wore.

"Damon? Hey. How are you feeling?"

Damon turned around, looking guilty. "Oh, Reg. Sorry, did I wake you up? I was trying to be quiet."

"No, it's okay. I would have been up soon anyway."

A lie, and he would know it was.

"Well… I made coffee. Can't start my day without one."

"Me neither." Reg watched the coffee maker drip into the pot.

The coffee smelled awfully good. Maybe that's why she had woken up. "So... how are you? Feeling better?"

"Pretty much back to normal. Davyn is a good healer; I'll say that for him."

The two warlocks were not exactly friends. Davyn was the leader of the main warlock coven in Black Sands, and at the opposite end of the spectrum, Damon wasn't even a member of any coven. He was a 'lone wolf,' a warlock who preferred to act on his own, without the rules or fellowship of a coven. Reg didn't know whether Davyn found that insulting, or if his personality was just too different from Damon's for them to get along and be friends. There was no animosity between them, as far as she could tell, but they weren't friends, and she didn't expect they ever would be.

"Yes. He's a good healer. And a good teacher. I enjoy it when he comes over to teach me something new or to help me to practice."

"I don't think you need a lot of direction." When Reg opened her mouth to object and to say that she hadn't known anything at all about firecasting before Davyn had come along, Damon waved her to silence. "I know what you were doing when I was in the conference center. I couldn't see it, exactly, but I could feel it. Powerful magic. We would never have survived if you hadn't been able to slow down the fire and stop it from reaching us. We didn't have a chance. The firefighters were amazed that we weren't dead by the time they got to us. Or at least incapacitated by the smoke. What you did was incredible. I've never heard of anything like that."

"It didn't feel like much," Reg confessed. "I mean, it was hard, yes, and it took a lot more energy than I had on hand. But it still felt like it was... I don't know... clunky. Clumsy. Like I was just playing around, and got lucky."

"That was not luck. That was skill. Davyn could not have done that. Him telling you not to practice firecasting while he's not here..." Damon snorted. "I don't know. It's like telling Einstein just to practice his times tables and not to try anything harder."

Reg thought that was a bit of an exaggeration. She rolled her eyes. Without saying anything else about it, she grabbed the full coffee pot and poured them each a mug. Starlight meowed and rubbed against her legs, so she fed him while she waited for her coffee to cool to a temperature where she could drink it.

"You slept okay? I doubt if that couch was very comfortable."

"Slept like the dead. Feel pretty good this morning, other than a bit of stiffness."

"Good. But don't plan on a repeat. I don't generally have men sleep over. Or have anyone sleeping on my couch. This is where I work."

He nodded. "Understood. It was just a one-time thing. I didn't actually intend to fall asleep there. It just happened."

"It's okay. I know you needed it. I wasn't about to wake you up and send you on your way. Just don't spread it around that you slept here. I don't think that my landlord would like it. Or certain other people."

"Why do you care what Corvin thinks?"

"I didn't say I was talking about Corvin."

"But you were."

Reg didn't bother to deny it. What was the point of lying to him when he knew as soon as she spoke whether she was telling the truth or not? If she denied it, she would just sound more pathetic.

Damon sipped his coffee. Reg added a bit of sugar to hers and looked in the fridge while she took her first couple of swallows. She had apparently finished off the ice cream the night before. Most of the food in the fridge had been there for a while, so she started to pull the oldest takeout containers out and drop them into the garbage. Sarah would be so impressed that she was actually initiating cleaning on her own. Starlight got in the way a few times, wanting to know what Reg was doing, then finally snorted in disgust and returned to Reg's bedroom for a nap.

In a few minutes, Reg was distracted from her cleaning by a knock on the door. She looked over at Damon and swore. She had not been planning on anyone else finding out that Damon had spent the night. Maybe it was just Davyn checking in on the two of them, but Reg doubted it. The door didn't open, so it wasn't Sarah.

Reg walked over and looked through the peephole. She swore again.

"Who is it?" Damon asked in a low voice.

"Vivian."

"What do you want me to do?"

Reg swore again. "I don't know."

"There isn't exactly anything wrong about me being here. And there's no reason to think that I slept over."

Reg looked pointedly at her housecoat.

"I might have been rude and come over early and gotten you out of bed," Damon suggested. "Like Vivian is doing."

Reg rubbed her forehead. "Fine. Go over and… plump up the cushions on the couch or something so it doesn't look slept in. And fix your hair."

Damon ran his fingers through his hair to tame his bed-head and went over to the couch. Reg took a couple of breaths and looked around for anything else that might be out of place. Vivian knocked on the door again. Reg sighed and let her in.

Vivian took in her state of dress. "Oh, did I get you up?"

"Seems like everyone is determined to get me up this morning," Reg said grumpily, shooting a look in Damon's direction. "I told you before I don't get up early."

Vivian looked at Damon and her eyes widened a little. "You're the guy who was at the conference center yesterday. You helped get that family out."

Damon nodded. "Couldn't do it myself, as it turned out, but I tried."

"I didn't see your car out front."

"It isn't parked out front."

If Vivian were fishing for information on whether Reg and Damon were in a relationship, she wasn't getting anything. Reg and Damon both waited for her to make the next move.

"I'm happy you were there to help." Vivian shifted uncomfortably. "I would have felt terrible if people had been killed in that… accident. I feel bad enough about the destruction and people who got hurt or scared."

"It wasn't exactly your fault, though, was it?" Reg asked. Without asking, she poured a cup of coffee for Vivian and handed it to her.

They all sat down. Reg and Damon sat on the couch, and Reg ended up closer to Damon than she had intended to. His leg brushed against hers, and she wondered whether he was intentionally teasing her or trying to make Vivian think they were a couple. She felt her face flush red but didn't say anything about it or make a show of moving away.

"No, but I know that things happen around me." Vivian wrapped her hands around her coffee mug like she was cold. She looked over at Damon, obviously not sure what to say in front of him.

"I filled in Damon on the basics," Reg told her. "After the fire. I figured he deserved to know what was going on, since it had affected him."

Vivian nodded and didn't seem upset about the disclosure. Reg was never sure what level of privacy was appropriate with a psychic client. But Vivian had been all over the news, so it wasn't like her accidents were a secret.

"I can't predict when something will happen…" Vivian explained, "but I try to stay away from places where other people might be hurt…"

"But you went to the conference center yesterday," Reg pointed out.

"I thought… with the accidents that have happened recently, it would be a while until the next thing… that I'd be safe for a while again…"

Reg sipped her coffee and waited. Vivian had said that the accidents were getting worse and closer together. She had to know that it wasn't safe for her to go anywhere.

"I just want… to have a normal life," Vivian said. "This has been going on for too long and I just want it all to end. I need to know what to do."

Reg looked at Damon to see if he had any input, then back at Vivian.

"If you want me to help you, or to try to help find a solution, then you need to be honest with me."

"I am."

"You've been holding things back from the start. Every time I learn something… you bolt. It's not helping us to solve anything. So… you need to tell me everything."

"I have."

"Why did you take off after Calliopia and Ruan were here?"

Vivian's lips pressed tightly together in a thin line. She shifted again and sipped her coffee. Her free hand went to her blouse, pressing against her chest. It looked like she was scared or cold, but Reg knew there was more to it.

"Your necklace. Was it something to do with your cat necklace?"

Vivian's hand closed around it, clutching it through her shirt where it was hidden. "No."

Reg looked at Damon, but didn't need his headshake to tell her that Vivian was lying. She shrugged. "If you don't tell me everything, I can't do anything to help you. Simple as that. I can't just guess what it is you need from me. I don't know how to get rid of this problem without being told all of the details. So… there's really no point in you coming back here over and over."

"But…"

Reg waited.

Vivian squeezed the cat pendant. "When you blessed that girl's cat pendant, or whatever it was you did, I thought it was all just show. But when you touched me… I felt something that I hadn't felt for a very, very long time."

Reg remembered brushing past Vivian when she had handed Calliopia's pendant back. Vivian had flinched back and had left soon after that without a good explanation. But Reg couldn't remember feeling anything unusual either while she was putting strength and healing into the necklace or after handing it over to Calliopia.

"What did you feel?"

"I don't know. Like… someone was talking to me. In a deep voice."

"A deep voice?" Reg couldn't keep the bewilderment out of her tone.

Vivian touched her head, scowling. "Not… deep in tone. But… like it was reaching inside of me. Like… important. Awe-inspiring."

Reg had no idea what that meant. Apparently, there was some

kind of connection between the two of them. Because Reg had read her a couple of times? Because she had seen the lion incident, the first strange accident that Vivian remembered? Had that put them on similar wavelengths somehow?

She hoped it didn't mean that she was now under the curse too.

"What if I touch you again," Reg suggested, "and we see if it happens again?"

Vivian was hesitant. "I don't know. I'm not here because of that."

"Really?"

"I… just want it to stop, and you're the only one that I feel like could help me. I've had all kinds of people who said that they could. Scammers who just wanted fame and fortune. But I feel like you understand, like you could do something. At least I know that you really have… second sight."

"Do you think I can help you without touching you?"

Vivian's face fell. She looked down. "No."

"Well, then?"

Vivian didn't reply for some time. Then she finally acquiesced. Her shoulders slumped down and she stared at the floor. "Okay. Fine."

Reg waited for her to do or say something else, and when Vivian didn't, Reg got up. She stepped around the coffee table so that she was at Vivian's side, and slowly reached out her hand to see if there was some sensation when she got close to Vivian, either warmth or a repelling force.

CHAPTER THIRTY-ONE

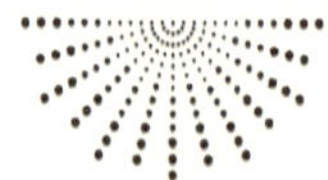

*N*othing happened.

Reg looked over at Damon, then back at Vivian. She closed the distance between them until they were just a hair's breadth apart. Still, nothing. She could feel the warmth of Vivian's body, but nothing unusual.

Carefully, Reg laid her hand on Vivian's shoulder.

Still nothing, but there was a layer of cloth between them. Reg moved her hand to Vivian's bare arm, prepared for something momentous to happen.

But still, there was nothing. She looked at Vivian's face to see if she were feeling anything. Maybe it was something that only the recipient felt. But Vivian just stared back at her, waiting for something to happen. Waiting for the voice to reach deep down inside her.

Eventually, Reg withdrew her hand. "Well, I guess it wasn't that. It must have been something else. Do you think it could have been the presence of Calliopia or Ruan? Did you feel anything particular toward either of them?"

"No. I thought… they were strange children. But other than that, no. Just that they were odd."

Reg nodded. Vivian didn't seem to have recognized them as a

fairy and a pixie. As far as she was concerned, there was nothing special about them.

"Well, maybe this, then. Where did you get the cat pendant? Do you think… it was something about Calliopia's pendant? About me…" Reg used Vivian's word, "…blessing it?"

"Maybe. But her cat… wasn't really anything like my cat."

Reg heard Starlight jump down from the bed or windowsill in the bedroom. She made the connection. "I was holding Starlight. And he had been helping with the pendant. Maybe he was what had an effect on you."

Vivian looked anxiously in Starlight's direction as he made his way across the cottage toward Reg. Calliopia had commented on what a powerful being Starlight was. Maybe she had seen something with her fairy sight that Reg could not. When Reg had looked at Starlight with her second sight, he had been a brilliant shining white. Reg took a deep breath and looked at Vivian, willing herself to see any spells or aura that she hadn't been able to see casually.

The pendant under Vivian's shirt was glowing. Vivian herself seemed dark and distant, but the cat pendant, like Starlight, was bright white, like a little star fallen right in the middle of Reg's cottage.

"Starlight." Reg called to him and he came over.

Vivian looked frightened. It would appear that she was not ready for the cat to touch her. She did not want to feel that voice calling to her again.

"Where did you get the necklace?" Reg asked.

Vivian covered it with her hand again, even though it was beneath her shirt. "I don't remember."

"Something like that? You must know where you got it. Is it a family heirloom?"

"Yes. I… my grandmother, great grandmother, I don't remember. It's been in my family for a long time."

Reg glanced at Damon. He didn't shake his head this time, just looked down. Reg still understood. *No.* Vivian was lying. Reg watched Starlight approach Vivian and sniffing the air. His pupils got big like they did when he was hunting or playing a chase game with her. He stalked Vivian, legs stiff and the fur on his back fluffed out.

Vivian shook her head. "I don't think he likes me. I don't want him to attack me again."

"He won't, will you Starlight? We just want to try an experiment, see whether it was Starlight that triggered a reaction before. Maybe that will help us to figure out what's going on with you."

"No. I don't think I want to do this." Vivian prepared to stand up.

"You said you wanted a normal life. Did you change your mind?"

Vivian hesitated. "No." She shook her head slightly. "I want... I want to be normal, like anyone else."

"Then let's figure this out. If it's something to do with cats, maybe that means it's something to do with your necklace."

"But what? That doesn't make any sense."

"It doesn't have to make sense. It's just suggestive. A parallel that might be worth looking into."

Vivian watched Starlight getting closer to her, holding tightly to her pendant.

"I don't want to talk to her."

Reg raised her brows. "To who? Starlight? He's a him, not a her."

"No. I think she's... he's..."

Reg looked at Starlight, curious about what he was going to do and what Vivian was so worried about. Maybe, like the fairies and pixies—and Corvin, for that matter—she hated cats instinctively. Could that be all it was?

Starlight stood up on his hind legs and put his front paws on Vivian's chair. Very delicately, he reached out one paw and tapped Vivian's leg.

Vivian's eyes rolled back and Reg stood, worried that she was going to faint and fall out of the chair. But by the time she could reach across the coffee table to steady Vivian, her eyes returned to their previous position. She looked straight at Reg, her pupils pinprick size, almost swallowed up by her brown irises.

Reg swallowed, her mouth suddenly dry.

"You should be careful of what you ask for," Vivian said, her voice deep, but devoid of emotion.

"Because you might get it," Reg finished. She remembered Harrison warning her about making wishes. And Sarah had said something soon after Reg had arrived in Black Sands, hadn't she? Something about how wishes granted by fairies in fairy tales always ended up backfiring on the wisher. Somehow, it always ended up getting twisted around so that it was something bad instead of what the wisher had actually wanted.

"What did you wish?" Damon asked.

Vivian continued to stare at Reg, eyes wide, but pupils constricted. She looked eerily like an addict, but Reg knew she hadn't taken anything.

"What did you wish on?" Reg asked. Was it a fairy wish? One of those falling-star or blow-out-a-candle wishes that little kids make? A wishing well or something else? A genie in a lamp?

Vivian pulled the cat pendant out, exposing it to their view. She let it lay in front of her shirt. Reg studied the glittering gold cat.

"Did you wish on the cat?"

Vivian nodded. Starlight let out a long, strange meow that raised the hair on the back of Reg's neck. Starlight sat on the floor beside Vivian's chair, straight and tall, looking directly at her the same way as Vivian was, except that his pupils were big, swallowing up his eyes with blackness. Reg had never been afraid of Starlight, but it was eerie.

"Where did you get it? It wasn't an heirloom."

"I found it."

"You found it?" Reg repeated. That was highly unlikely. One of those things that people said when they didn't want to be called out as a thief. So who had Vivian stolen it from? Was that why she was now under a curse?

"When I was digging." Vivian's voice was childlike. Reg remembered the little girl who was stolen away by the lion. "I was digging on my site. Like Daddy."

"You said your father was an archaeologist," Reg remembered. But then she heard Vivian's actual words in her mind. He was *like* an archaeologist. What was like an archaeologist? Someone who dug up artifacts in northern Africa?

Not an archaeologist.

A treasure hunter. A tomb raider.

They had become very comfortable. He'd made good money plundering, enough to support his family and raise their status in the world.

"In northern Africa?" Reg asked. "You found the cat when you were digging in northern Africa?"

Vivian nodded slowly, her face expressionless.

"Where, exactly?"

She anticipated the answer before Vivian said it. "Egypt."

Egypt. A land filled with the tombs of rich Pharaohs. Reg didn't know if she believed that Vivian had just discovered the pendant while digging in the sand. Maybe it was in one of the tombs her father plundered. Maybe her father hadn't even seen it, didn't know that she had gone in and taken it.

Everyone knew that the treasures in a mummy's tomb were cursed.

That was why Vivian kept having near-death experiences.

She had stolen a cursed treasure.

CHAPTER THIRTY-TWO

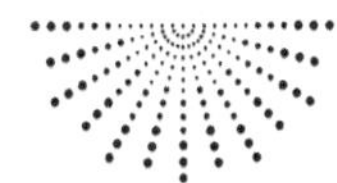

But Reg knew there was more to it than that. Finding a cursed treasure was dramatic enough, but there had to be more to it.

Because Vivian hadn't died. She hadn't come down with some unusual illness and died within weeks of the tomb being plundered. She had not died when the lion had stolen into the camp and tried to drag her away. She hadn't been killed in any of the incidents since then. Not when her house was crushed or when a truck came barreling down the street with her directly in its path.

Vivian had mentioned a wish. Be careful what you wish for…

"What did you wish?"

There was a long period of silence and Reg wondered whether Vivian were going to answer. She seemed to be half in a trance; able to answer Reg's questions, but flat and distant, no emotion in her words.

"I wished… that I would be young forever. That I never had to get old and die."

Vivian touched the cat pendant. A shadow passed over her face and, for a split-second, Reg saw an illusion. Vivian, her face wrinkled and ancient. Small and sunken and withered like a mummy. No flesh, just dried, wrinkled skin over a skull.

Reg gasped and blinked, and the illusion was gone. She was, once again, gazing at Vivian's smooth, unblemished, unwrinkled face.

"When was that? How long ago?"

Vivian's head moved from side to side. "Too long to count… I was just a little girl at the time. In Egypt…"

"You must know about how long ago it was. What year was it? What else was going on in the world?"

"I don't know. I only knew my own little world… just my family, and whatever camp or village we were in."

"You must have heard things on the TV or radio. Someone must have had a radio."

Damon made a small noise. Reg looked at him, but he didn't say anything. Reg looked back at Vivian. How old could she be? Detective Jessup said that Sarah was centuries old. Sarah said she had seen Vivian somewhere before. Vivian couldn't be older than Sarah.

"There were no radios," Vivian said. "No. Not for a long, long time."

"Well… what about wars? Who was fighting? What kind of people were in Egypt?"

Vivian shook her head. "Egyptians. I never saw a white face. Never heard another language."

Reg looked at Damon, hoping that he would help her. She had not done well in history in school. She'd never been able to keep everything straight and in order or to remember what happened in what years. But what Vivian described sounded far more ancient than anything she had learned about.

"But… back before… you know, BC, there were Romans in Egypt, weren't there? She would have heard whatever they spoke."

"Maybe not out in the desert," Damon said. "In the big cities and trade centers, maybe, but if she was only living in small camps and villages out in the desert, she might have been very isolated. Even in modern times."

"I don't think… she's modern," Reg said quietly. She didn't like discussing Vivian as if she weren't right there in the room, but the Vivian they had talked to seemed very far away, and she didn't react to their words unless they addressed her directly. Reg couldn't get that ancient, wrinkled face out of her head. If that was how Vivian was supposed to look, if she had aged and died the way she was supposed to, then she had to be very old. More than a hundred. More than Sarah.

"Help me," Vivian pled. Her pupils were still pinpricks. "Help me to break the curse."

"You want the accidents to stop," Reg agreed.

"No… No."

"Do you know anything about breaking curses?" Reg asked Damon. "Ancient Egyptian curses?"

Damon shook his head. "No, I'm not the one to ask. That's way outside my wheelhouse."

"Who, then? Sarah? Corvin?"

"Maybe Sarah," Damon said uncertainly. "But I'm not sure how much she will know… or remember. And Corvin, he only knows what he's studied over the years. Maybe he's come across something in some ancient scrolls, but… he's not old enough to *remember* anything like that."

Reg needed someone older. Someone who had been around not just for decades or centuries, but thousands of years.

* * *

Reg looked at Starlight, thinking it through, examining the idea from several angles before speaking.

"Then maybe… Harrison."

Damon raised an eyebrow. He had met Harrison a couple of times briefly, but only knew as much about him and the others who claimed to be immortals as anyone else.

"He would know, right?" Reg asked.

"Maybe. Your guess is as good as mine. Probably better. But you'd have to get him to come here, and then to explain what it is that you want from him, and then to get him to do it…" Damon trailed off.

And he was right, of course. Talking to Harrison was one thing; actually communicating with him and getting him to do something helpful was quite another.

"Harrison?" Reg repeated. She focused on how he had looked the last time she had seen him, happily eating ribs with Starlight.

And there was another connection with Starlight. If Starlight was connected with Harrison, and was somehow connected with Vivian or the pendant, then what did that tell Reg about him? Harrison had referred to Starlight as an old friend.

How old?

"Is it a party?" Harrison asked. "I didn't bring a gift."

Reg opened her eyes and looked at Harrison, standing behind Starlight. He was wearing a bright red satiny shirt and played with his luxurious mustache while he looked at her, smiling.

"Don't play games with me," Reg said. "You can make a gift appear whenever you like. You don't have to bring it with you."

"This is true," Harrison agreed, nodding sagely. He looked around. "But if it is a party, there should be cake."

And there was, on the kitchen island. A beautiful black forest cake with curls of dark chocolate and bright red cherries and mounds of creamy icing. Reg's mouth began to water. She tried to remind her body that it was first thing in the morning and she hadn't even finished her coffee yet. She certainly wasn't ready to dig into a big chocolate cake. She shook her head at Harrison.

"What's with the obsession with food?" she demanded.

Harrison shrugged. "It is one of the few pleasures in taking on a human body."

Reg supposed he had a point there. "Well… you can have some cake in a minute. First… I need some help."

Harrison looked around again, studying Damon and then Vivian. "You do not appear to be in any danger."

"No, I'm not." Unless Vivian's bad luck were to strike while she was still in Reg's cottage. She didn't feel like being crushed by a boulder or tree or blown to kingdom come. "It's a problem with a client. We wanted to know… how to break the curse that is on her." Reg gestured to Vivian.

Harrison looked at Vivian again. "What curse?"

"Can't you see it? She's been cursed with…" Reg felt a little ridiculous putting it into words. "Staying young and living forever."

"I thought this was mankind's ultimate wish."

"Well… I guess it was Vivian's wish… but she doesn't want it anymore. She wants to live a normal life. All of these terrible things keep happening around her because… I guess… fate knows that she should have been dead a long time ago."

Harrison nodded. "Of course."

"Well… she doesn't want those things to keep happening. She wants to just be a normal human being, with a normal length of life."

"She cannot. She has already far surpassed that."

"Well, I mean, from now. For her to just live a normal human lifespan after today."

Harrison scratched his head, thinking about this. "I do not know," he said slowly.

"You can do anything. You're immortal."

"Immortal isn't the same as omnipotent," Damon reminded Reg. "There may be a lot of things that your Uncle Harrison can do, but he can't do anything."

Reg scowled. "As far as I am concerned, he can do anything."

Harrison smiled sunnily. "You see?" he said to Damon. "That's why she is my goddaughter."

"She isn't."

"Well, she could be."

"Guys, guys," Reg waved her hands at them. "Cut it out. Harrison. Can you remove the curse?"

"It is not a curse," he corrected. "It is a granted wish."

"Then can you remove the granted wish?"

He shook his head slowly. "One cannot remove a granted wish. It is already granted."

"She doesn't want to be immortal."

"She is not."

"If she stays young and lives forever, then she is immortal," Reg insisted. She looked at Damon. "Right? I got it right that time?"

"Yeah. That's kind of the definition of immortal," Damon informed Harrison.

Harrison *tsked* and brushed this off with a hand motion. "She is human. She is not one of my kind."

"Maybe not, but she's still immortal, and she doesn't want to be anymore. She wants to age normally and then die at the end of her lifespan."

Harrison looked at Vivian. He shook his head again, as if they were being silly. "She does not want that."

"Tell him, Vivian," Reg told the woman, who was just sitting there like a statue as they discussed her fate.

"No," Vivian said, stone-faced.

Reg sat there with her mouth open.

Harrison nodded at Reg and folded his arms over his chest. "You see? She does not want that."

"Vivian." Reg stared into Vivian's eyes, trying to connect with her to make sure that she understood what Reg was saying. "Vivian. You asked me to help you. I'm trying to help you. But you have to tell Harrison that it's what you want. You want to age and live a normal life, right? That's what you said."

Vivian shook her head slowly. Her pupils grew slightly so that Reg hoped she was coming out of the trance and could communicate more clearly. "I don't want to age," she said. "I don't want to live a normal lifespan."

"But you said…"

"I want to die."

Reg stared at her. "What?"

Vivian blinked a few times, her eyes growing more normal. She looked down at Starlight, and then up over her shoulder at the gangly, brightly-dressed Harrison.

"I can't keep living like this, plodding through life year after year after year. All of these near-death encounters. It's like life is taunting me. I want to die. I want it to finally be over."

"But you said you wanted to live a normal life."

"Is my life normal? If you stood in the path of a speeding truck, would it swerve around you at the last moment?" Vivian demanded. "Because of a little rock in the road? You told me that if I did not want to die, I needed to step out of the path of the truck. But you were wrong. I didn't step out of the path, and it didn't kill me. And neither did the lion, or the boulder, or the airplane, or the bomb, or the tornado…"

Reg looked for something to say. "But you just want those things to stop happening, don't you? Just to…"

"I don't need them to stop. If they do stop, I don't care, as long as I can put a pistol to my head and pull the trigger!"

"You see?" Harrison asked reasonably. "She does not want—"

"Yes, I get it," Reg snapped. "You were right. I get it. But she does want the curse to be removed. The wish. She wants it taken away."

"She wants to die," Harrison said, shaking his head slightly. "You have rules. You do not want me to kill your friends or to do anything that results in their deaths."

"No," Reg agreed slowly, trying to feel her way through his argument. "I don't want that… normally… but Vivian isn't a friend, she is a client, and she came to me because she wants the granted wish removed. So that she can die if she wants to."

Harrison wandered over to the cake and stuck his finger into the icing. He scooped out a generous amount of icing and stuck his finger in his mouth.

"Harrison…"

"Maybe she hasn't tried hard enough," Harrison suggested.

"Tried hard enough to what? To kill herself?"

He nodded.

"I think she's tried hard enough," Reg said. "Did you hear about all of the things she has been through? And I'm sure there are plenty more she hasn't even mentioned."

"Accidents," Harrison pointed out. "That's not trying."

Reg looked at Vivian, at a loss for words. Vivian looked at Harrison, her brows drawn down.

"Who are you, anyway? And who are you to say that I haven't tried? I've done everything I could to die. Poison. Jumping off a bridge. Shooting or stabbing myself. Getting other people to shoot me… you don't know how many different things I have tried, and it never works."

Harrison nodded. He looked through Reg's drawers and eventually found a large serving fork, which he used to cut a wedge of cake.

He ate it off of the fork, shoving it messily into his mouth. He stood there wiping the icing off of his face with his finger and then licking his finger off like a cat.

Reg looked down at Starlight. "Harrison…"

"Yeph?"

"Who is Starlight? Is he an immortal like you?"

Harrison considered the question for a moment. Reg could guess what he was going to say before it came out of his mouth. The only thing he could say to muddy the waters even further.

"Not like me, no."

"Is he an immortal?"

Harrison rubbed his thumb over his lip, looking down at his furry friend. "He is a cat."

"I know that. But is he an immortal that has taken cat form, like you take human form?"

"Not like me—"

"Oh, you are the most irritating… Is he a real cat?"

Harrison nodded. "Most definitely."

"Has he always been a cat?"

"Always?" Harrison stared off into space. "Always… no."

"What was he before he was a cat?"

Harrison closed his eyes momentarily, grimacing like he was coming down with a migraine. "Humans have such a narrow view of temporal time…"

Reg fixed her eyes on Starlight, trying to hold his gaze. She could feel his emotions. She couldn't interpret his thoughts into English language, but she understood his feelings and what he wanted. Usually.

"Star, can you help me? Can you do something here? She is wearing a cat necklace, and she wished on it, and you have… some kind of connection with her. Do you know her? From… before? Sometime? Somewhere?"

He gazed back at her. How did she expect him to answer such a complex thought? Even if he did, how would he answer it with a single thought or emotion?

"Can you change her? Can you…" Reg had been about to ask if

he could take the wish away, but Harrison had already said that the wish, once granted, couldn't be taken away. It was, if Reg understood, in the past, and that could not change. But Harrison had taken her into the past before and things had changed. Maybe it was more than that. One of those rules that the immortals were not supposed to break. No takesie backsies on wishes. "Can you *change* her wish?"

Starlight cocked his head at Reg. She always thought it was so cute when he tried to figure something out and tilted his head to the side like that when curious or puzzled.

"Come on, Starlight," she encouraged. "Can you change Vivian's wish?"

He looked at Vivian. Vivian shifted away slightly, still uncertain about the cat.

Starlight jumped up into her lap.

CHAPTER THIRTY-THREE

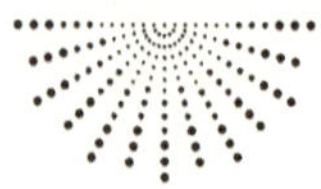

$\mathcal{V}$ ivian gave a little shriek of surprise, and moved to push him off of her lap. Starlight dug his claws in. Reg winced, knowing what it was like to try to move him if he didn't want to move.

"Let him be," she told Vivian. "Don't you want him to help?"

"No," Vivian cried. But she wasn't speaking to Reg; she was looking at Starlight, who held her fixed in his gaze. "Please, I didn't mean any harm. I just want… I want it to be over. Don't you think I've paid enough?"

Starlight looked into her eyes. He pawed at the cat necklace.

"Maybe you should take it off," Reg suggested, trying to think of what Starlight might be telling her to do. "Have you ever tried that?"

"Have I ever taken it off?" Vivian shot back. "Of course I've taken it off! But it's mine. I want it close to me. It's been a part of me for so long."

"It's not part of you. It's a necklace. And if it's what you wished on, it's what is causing the curse, then if you took it off and destroyed it—"

Starlight's head whipped around and he hissed at her. Reg jumped, startled by the vehemence of his reaction.

"Oh, okay. Not destroy it." They'd had to unmake Calliopia's knife in order for her to be able to heal, so she had immediately jumped to the wrong conclusion. "Sorry."

Harrison was watching Reg curiously, still picking at the chocolate cake and licking his fingers.

"Something else. Maybe you need to take it back to where you got it. It isn't really yours. It was someone else's and maybe you weren't supposed to disturb it."

"If I don't have this necklace…" Vivian grasped it in her hand. She struggled for words. "I need it. It's part of me."

"Maybe that's the part that needs to be taken away if you want to remove the curse. The wish. Maybe that's the part of you that's holding on to it."

Vivian tried a couple of times to lift Starlight off of her lap, detaching all of his claws from her clothes, before she succeeded in separating him. She put him down on the floor and stood up.

"I came to you for help!" she told Reg, "I thought that maybe you could help me. I should have known as soon as I saw your cat that you wouldn't do anything for me. Bastet would never let you help me. She wants me to suffer."

"Starlight is a boy. He. And he's not Bastet."

Starlight, who had been licking his fur down firmly after Vivian had handled him, stopped and looked at Reg. Reg shook her head, frowning. "You can't be Bastet."

His eyes didn't move away from her.

"But… Bastet was female," Reg said lamely.

Harrison started to laugh. Reg shot him an angry look. "Not helpful, Harrison!"

"Male and female," Harrison chuckled. "As if those were the only two choices! Humans…"

"Well, those are the only two flavors that cats come in," Reg snapped. "And Bastet, the Egyptian god, was definitely a female. A goddess."

"How do you know?"

"Because that's the way she's portrayed in all of the statues. A woman. A cat with kittens. She's the goddess of fertility and all that."

"Were you there?"

"Where?"

"Egypt."

"When they worshiped Bastet? No."

"Immortals can take many forms. The… outside," Harrison made a motion to indicate his body. "The *shell*, it does not always represent the… essence."

"So Bastet wasn't female? Is Starlight Bastet? How could he be?"

"You can accept that your Starlight's true form might not be a cat?"

"Yes."

"But not that Starlight's inside could be different than Starlight's outside?"

Reg ground her knuckle into her forehead. "Okay. Of course. But he is… thousands of years old? I know you said he was an old friend, but he couldn't be… he couldn't be an ancient Egyptian god, could he?"

Starlight marched over to Reg and sat at her feet. He drew himself up into a tall sitting position, giving a little quiver from his body up to his ears. He blinked at her with his blue and green eyes. Reg held her hand out to him and he rubbed against her, just as he always did. Reg couldn't wrap her mind around the idea that Starlight could be some ancient being who had been worshiped thousands of years ago.

He was a cat. Her cat. They had chosen each other.

He liked fish and chicken.

She cleaned his litter box.

"I won't give up my necklace," Vivian said sullenly, bringing Reg back to the matter at hand.

"Then I don't think there's any hope of you shedding the curse. If you want to change, then you have to give up that part of you." Reg looked at Harrison. "Is that right?"

"Humans are changeable," Harrison said agreeably, "even if they think they are not. To remove a wish, one must remove it. From the inside and the outside." He nodded to Vivian.

"It's up to you," Reg said to Vivian. "You said you wanted to change. Do you really?"

She had been expecting something dramatic. A blinding flash of light and the curse or wish would be removed. Vivian might melt like the Wicked Witch of the West into a pile of mummy dust, but it was what she wanted, so that would be okay. After the dramatic finales in other cases, she had thought this one would be spectacular.

Vivian stood there, considering, looking absolutely miserable. "I don't even know where to take it. It was so long ago, and the whole face of the land has changed. I can't return it to where I got it. It's probably under some freeway now."

"Does she want to return it?" Harrison asked the air.

Reg looked at him, then looked at Vivian.

"Maybe you could give it to Starlight," she said. "If he's Bastet, and it represents him… if he's the one who granted the wish…"

Vivian shook her head. "You would like that, wouldn't you? This whole thing was just to talk me into handing over a priceless solid gold artifact to your cat? So that you can cash in on it?"

Reg shrugged. She wasn't sure she wanted the pendant in her house anyway. It certainly hadn't brought Vivian the happiness she had predicted. Reg didn't want it around if it brought bad luck. She had all of the wealth she needed.

"I don't want it. It was just a suggestion."

"You don't want it? Who do you think you're kidding? Everybody wants it. Everybody who sees it, their eyes light up and they start thinking of ways to get their hands on it. Do you know how many people have tried to murder me to get it? Which is really ironic, since it won't let anyone kill me!"

Vivian rolled the cat back and forth in her hand, studying it, unable to make the decision that would free her from its spell.

"I wish someone would just take it from me. I don't care what they did with it. Keep it, sell it, take it back to Egypt. Make their own wishes and wander like a ghost for thousands of years trying to escape its curse. I wish someone would just take it away!"

Harrison walked over to Vivian. He grasped the pendant, yanked on it to break the gold chain it hung on, and vanished from sight.

Vivian screamed. It had all happened so quickly; she hadn't known what it was Harrison was doing. She caught the empty chain as it fell from her neck and held it in both hands, shrieking.

"No! No, no, no!"

"Be careful what you wish for," Damon said from the couch.

"No!" Vivian whipped around to face him, her face a mask of horror, more dramatic than any Reg had seen on late-night TV movies. "I didn't! I didn't wish it. I didn't want it! Make him come back!"

She turned to Reg.

"Please! Call him back. Make him bring it back; this isn't what I wanted!"

Reg shook her head. "I can't control him."

And she didn't want to call him back. She didn't want to give Vivian the opportunity to change her mind. She had come to have the wish removed, and if that was what Harrison had done, then no matter how devastated Vivian appeared to be, Reg had to believe it would work out and Vivian would eventually be able to come to terms with what had happened. It had been what she wanted, even if she had been shocked by the suddenness of it.

"You witch!" Vivian shouted. "You made me come here, put a spell on me, and stole my necklace! I'm going to report you! You can't do this to me! You can't!"

She darted toward Starlight, and Reg stepped forward to stop her, worried she was going to kick the cat or do something else that might seriously injure him. But Starlight was faster than Vivian and jumped out of the way. He managed to gouge the backs of her calves as he ran around her. Vivian howled and looked at the claw marks as they started to bleed.

"I'll have him put down! You have a vicious animal! I'll call animal control and they'll take him away!"

"Maybe you should leave now," Damon suggested.

Vivian gave him a long, icy glare, and then marched out of the cottage, slamming the door behind her.

CHAPTER THIRTY-FOUR

Reg let out her breath. Well, if she'd wanted drama, she had gotten it. She looked at Damon, not sure what to do next.

"What if she does report Starlight?"

"She attacked him. I'll tell them that."

"But what if they don't believe us?" Reg picked Starlight up and held him close. He rubbed his head against the underside of her chin.

"It was a scratch. They don't destroy cats for scratching. All cats scratch."

Reg rubbed Starlight's ears.

Damon looked around. "At least Harrison left the cake," he observed.

Reg looked at the cake, which looked like it had been pecked by crows or a toddler had face-planted into it. Or both. There were a few areas left untouched. They could get a couple of slices out of it. And after the morning she'd had, she deserved it.

There was a loud rumbling sound and the floor shook under Reg's feet. Starlight wriggled to be put down and she let him go rather than be raked by his powerful hind legs. Starlight ran to the window and jumped up to look out.

There was a crashing, booming sound, and the vibrations under her feet subsided. Reg looked at Damon, feeling a chill.

"Was that an earthquake?"

"I don't know. It sure felt like one."

Reg remembered the feeling of the truck in her vision barreling toward Vivian and the crash that had shaken the house when she was at Francesca's.

"Oh, no."

She ran to the door and opened it. Of course, she could see nothing from her doorway. She looked over her shoulder to Damon.

"Shut the door behind you. Don't let Starlight get out."

Reg ran down the pathway to the front of the big house and looked around. People were starting to gather a block away. Reg bit her lip and prayed it wasn't another truck accident, and that if it were, no one else had been hurt. She hurried toward the gathering crowd at a fast walk, unable to run the whole way.

When she got there, there was no truck to be seen. There was little to see but a hole in the ground. A huge hole across the road, sidewalk, and part of someone's yard, that had to measure twenty feet across. Reg got closer, but she wasn't at the front of the crowd and she couldn't see the bottom of the hole.

"What is it? What happened?"

"Sinkhole," a bystander advised. "We get them sometimes in Florida. Something about the acid rain and limestone."

Reg strained for a better look. Then she looked at the faces of the crowd, looking for Vivian. Vivian would have been able to hear what had happened even more easily than Reg and Damon. She would have run over to see the sinkhole. But her face was not in the crowd.

"Was there... anybody there? Was anyone hurt?"

There was some back and forth in the crowd.

"I did see a woman here a few minutes before... but she must have gotten away. No one could be that unlucky..."

* * *

Reg started back to the house. She met Damon partway there. He saw her coming and stopped to wait, his eyes past her on the crowd.

"So... what happened?"

"Sinkhole."

"Oh. We do get a good number of those in Florida. Low water table. Eroding limestone."

"I think… Vivian is gone."

"You're not sure?"

"No one saw her fall into it… but a couple of people did say that they saw her, and she wasn't there in the crowd. If she saw the sinkhole collapse, she would have stayed around for a look like everyone else, wouldn't she?"

"Maybe. Maybe she's seen so many of them in her lifetime that she wouldn't."

"Still… the timing… I think fate finally succeeded in ending her life."

Damon nodded and didn't disagree. Sarah was coming out of the big house when they approached.

"Reg? What happened? Was it an earthquake?"

"A sinkhole."

"Oh. We haven't had one of those so close before." Sarah shook her head. "So many things have been happening in Black Sands the last few days. Just look at that fire! I can't believe that the two of you…" Sarah trailed off. "I saw it on TV. I'm so glad that you weren't badly hurt, Damon."

Damon nodded to Reg. "Thanks to Reg."

Sarah looked at Reg curiously. "Oh…?"

Reg shrugged modestly. "Well, I did what I could."

"Well, a good thing you were there. They say these things happen in threes, so I don't know whether the sinkhole is the beginning of a new set…"

"I don't think so. I think… that will be it for a while. Things should go back to normal soon."

"As normal as things ever are in Black Sands," Sarah laughed.

EPILOGUE

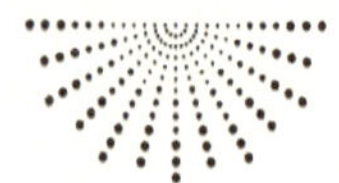

Reg hadn't heard from Corvin for a few days, which was unusual. Usually, he kept in pretty close touch, calling her or texting her late at night when it was quiet and she didn't have any clients. Nights she did have clients, he was pretty good at staying out of the way and letting her operate.

So when the doorbell rang, Reg didn't think of Corvin, but thought maybe it was a delivery from Amazon that she'd forgotten about or an unscheduled client. She swung the door open without checking the peephole first, and then stood there looking at Corvin, wondering what to do.

Slam the door in his face? Tell him to go home and call her? He was there. It would be stupid of her not to deal with him. Avoiding him wouldn't accomplish anything.

"Corvin. Hi."

He leaned on the doorway. "Regina."

Reg shivered. She didn't invite him in, but she didn't tell him to go home, either.

"I thought maybe you had decided it was best not to see me anymore."

"Why would I think that?"

"It would be less dangerous."

"Why would I want less dangerous?" His eyes glittered as he studied her.

Reg couldn't help smiling at that. She remembered how it had been when she first met him. Before she knew about what he could do. He had been intriguing, handsome and smooth, and everyone had told her to steer clear of him. So, of course, she hadn't. Reg Rawlins didn't listen to anyone else's advice. She only did what she thought was best. And Corvin, attractive, charming, always saying the right things and romancing her, had been an easy choice.

"Can Regina come out to play?" Corvin asked, smiling.

Reg looked behind her as if she had to check with someone, but she didn't. Starlight was snoozing on the bed, so even he couldn't hiss at her and stalk around disapprovingly.

"I guess I can come out," she agreed. She stepped out the door and motioned to the garden in the back. It was a pleasant night, warm with a bit of a breeze blowing in off the ocean. Reg could smell the salty tang of the ocean. She felt drawn to it. She wanted to go there. To take Corvin there. Finish what they had started.

Reg shook her head at this. She and Corvin sat down in the garden, where the only body of water was a tiny goldfish pond. He'd have to be completely unconscious for Reg to drown him in that. And even then, she wasn't sure.

"You didn't want to go back to the marina?" She teased. They were sharing a bench, but Reg was careful to leave a space between them. No need to touch or be breathing the same air. If he started to charm her, she was strong enough to resist.

"Uh, no. I think it's going to be a while before I go back there."

"Well, when you do, be sure to give me a call."

Corvin chuckled. "Does that mean you've come to terms with your siren nature?"

"No." Reg shook her head definitely. "I'm just teasing."

"You are what you are. You can't change that."

"I think people can always change. Saying that you can't is a cop-out."

"You can't change your DNA. The stuff that makes you. You can't change what's written there, the genetic memory, the instincts. And you can't change what happened in the past. The way that you grew up."

"Actually, I can," Reg reminded him. "I already did."

Corvin made a face and shook his head. "No. You changed some things about your past, yes, but you didn't manage to change the way that you were raised. All of the time you lived with Norma Jean, that didn't change. And all of the foster homes and moving around, that didn't change. The only thing that changed was that she didn't die."

Reg considered this. She had been surprised at how little had changed when she discovered that Norma Jean was still alive. She had always thought that if her mother hadn't died, her life would be completely different. And yet, it wasn't. It was still the same. Except that she'd had to face her mother, confront all of those issues, find out who her mother really was. And none of that had been any fun.

"I wish I could be like Harrison."

"What do you mean?"

"He can just go wherever he wants to, do whatever he wants to. He doesn't have to be human, but he can choose to be. He can eat whatever he wants and never put on weight. He can just... have a good time."

"And do you think he does?"

Reg thought about it, about everything she knew about Harrison. It actually wasn't very much. She only saw him occasionally when she called him or he chose to visit her. She only saw him when he was relaxed and enjoying himself. That didn't mean that's the way it always was. He could be off fighting dragons and sea monsters the rest of the time. She had no idea what his life was like when he wasn't with her.

"I don't know. I guess I never asked."

"Then you should be careful what you wish for."

"Yeah." Reg sighed. Why did it always keep coming back to that? Was there always a negative to every positive? For every good thing a person wished for, was there always something horrible lurking on the flip side? "Who would have thought that wishing to stay young forever would end up being a bad thing."

"There is danger in trying to change the natural order of things."

"I guess. But does that mean we shouldn't try? What about with Calliopia? Everyone was resigned to the fact that she was going to die, but she didn't have to. There was a way to save her. What if there is a way to change the things we want to, if we just try hard enough?"

Corvin stared off into the distance. Reg watched the flowers and leaves fluttering in the breeze. Neither of them said anything for a long time.

"Maybe there is," Corvin said finally. "But you have to want it badly enough."

Did you enjoy this book? Reviews and recommendations are vital to making a book successful.

Please leave a review at your favorite book store or review site and share it with your friends.

Don't miss the following bonus material:
Sign up for mailing list to get a free ebook
Read a sneak preview chapter
Other books by P.D. Workman
Learn more about the author

STEP DEEPER INTO BLACK SANDS

Step deeper with Reg Rawlins into the mystical town of Black Sands

Reg Rawlins never thought she'd stay in Black Sands.
What started as a simple con turned into something else—strange cases,
impossible choices, and a town where the usual rules don't apply.

If you want more, you can explore Reg's cases in a different way:

🔮 Ask the Crystal Ball

Find out which case you should read next

🃏 Draw a Card

Discover strange people, impossible situations, and dangerous choices

Get Exclusive Access

Special content, new releases, and reader-only extras

Welcome to Reg Rawlins's World

SKUNK MAN SWAMP

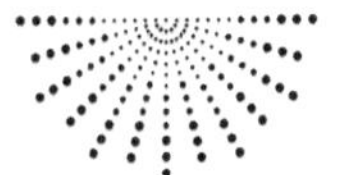

REG RAWLINS, PRIVATE INVESTIGATOR #10

CHAPTER ONE

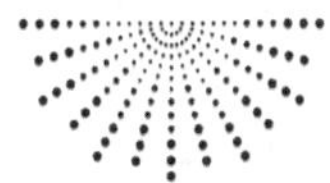

Reg realized she had become distracted and stopped hearing Damon. He had been talking about the Spring Games—apparently the magical equivalent of the Olympics—at least since Yule, but over the past few weeks it had become more and more central to his conversation, until it was practically the only thing he talked about. And she couldn't listen for long before tuning him out and going on a little mental vacation. Normally, she was good at looking attentive but this time she had apparently failed.

Damon was looking at her in exasperation, waiting for her to say something. His dark eyes drilled into her. She wasn't sure if he had asked a question or told a story that demanded some kind of polite social response. She searched his face for some clue. His dark eyes drilled into her. The reddening aura around his head told her that he was angry. Damon was usually laid back. It took a lot of provocation —or Corvin—to get him angry.

"I'm sorry," she said, hoping that an apology would get her out of this. "I got distracted. You were talking about the Spring Games…?"

What else would he have been talking about?

"Yes, I was," he agreed. "But I guess you're not interested."

"I'm interested," Reg objected immediately. "I was just thinking about something else. A client," she bluffed. "This one has me a little puzzled."

He gazed at her for another moment. Being a diviner, he would know she was lying, even though Reg was a good liar with plenty of practice. Her face warmed and she wished she could stop the blush.

"So, you are interested?"

Interested in what? In the Spring Games?

"Of course. Just tell me that last little bit again."

Damon scratched the stubbly whiskers of his goatee. He was handsome. Dark hair and eyes. Like Corvin, and yet nothing like Corvin. She couldn't compare her magnetic attraction to Corvin to her friendship with Damon. Damon's physical appearance couldn't compete with Corvin's magical charms.

"There are some indications that he could be in the Everglades," Damon told her.

"In the Everglades." Reg repeated this part of the statement, rather than asking, *Who?* She was clearly supposed to know who he was talking about.

"That's right. So I figured that you could help me find him with your psychic abilities, and I would split the reward with you. It would be a real coup to get him to the Games."

Reg's head spun. She had no clue who he was talking about or what it had to do with the Spring Games. She shook her head, her red box-braids swishing around her face. "You want me to go to the Everglades to find this guy?"

"Well, unless you can look in your crystal ball here and just tell me where he is. Yes. I want you to go with me to the Everglades to find the missing wizard."

Reg rubbed her temples. She looked over to her crystal ball on the shelf, considering. She could try seeking whoever this missing wizard was in her crystal ball. It was possible she would be successful. But if she did something as simple as that, would Damon still feel like she had earned half of the reward? He made it sound like he was expecting it to be quite a bit of money.

Reg had the money she needed. In fact, she hadn't shared the gems that she had received from Calliopia Papillon's parents with those who had helped her on her quest to save Calliopia. She hadn't even *told* the others in her company about the gift. Reg had learned the value of money during the lean years, when she had struggled to keep a roof over her head and food in her belly. She didn't like to think of herself as a selfish person, but she couldn't think of any other way to spin the fact that she had decided to keep all of the reward for herself.

Of course, the more people who knew about the gems, the higher the chances that someone would break into her cottage or attack her in order to get them. Valuable, easily transportable goods that could not be traced were a burglar's dream. Reg really should get a safety deposit box in a bank rather than leave them in the little wooden box under her bed.

But the crystal ball might be a way for her to find out more about the missing wizard Damon was talking about without letting on that she had been ignoring him. She stretched her stiff limbs. She had been sitting in the wicker chair listening to Damon go on about the Spring Games for too long. She made her way across the room to get her crystal ball from the shelf. She put it on the coffee table as she sat back down.

Damon watched her, looking slightly amused. Did he sense that this was just a ploy? She had to assume that he was taking her at face value and couldn't know what she was thinking. He could put visions into her head, but he couldn't read what she was thinking independently of him. Reg rubbed her hands together as if trying to warm them up.

"Starlight?" she called. "Do you want to join me?"

She heard her familiar jump down from the window in the bedroom, and the black and white tuxedo cat came padding out to see her. He blinked at her, first his blue eye and then his green one. He looked at Damon and rotated his ears around so they were facing backward. He didn't usually object to Damon, so Starlight either didn't appreciate her waking him up to participate in the impromptu reading—which, admittedly, Reg did not need her familiar for—or he could read the room and knew that Reg was anxious and Damon angry.

"Come on, Starlight," she invited. "Help me focus on the crystal."

He sat and washed. Reg waited. Rushing him or picking him up would not help. If he had decided he needed to wash before the reading, then he needed to wash before the reading. She had to respect his process. There was no way he was getting around it anyway.

Damon rolled his eyes. "Why don't you just go ahead?"

"No. I'll wait until he's ready."

They both watched Starlight, who gave no indication that he was going to be finished any time soon.

"Why don't you tell me a little more about this wizard while we're waiting?"

She mentally patted herself on the back for this stroke of brilliance. He would give her more detail, and she would be able to fill in the parts of the conversation she had missed and decide whether she were going to do anything more for him than just look in the crystal.

Damon stared up at the ceiling. "I'm not sure how much I can tell you or how useful it will be. I know his name, like I said, Jeffrey Wilson. He's a brilliant wizard, but he just dropped out of sight. No one knows where he went. But there is a reward for finding him and getting him to attend at the Spring Games and I thought… why not? I'll bet that you could find him, and it would be great publicity for both of us, me with my security business and you with your psychic stuff. And it pays well. I might not be able to pay you an hourly rate, but if you take it on contingency, I'll give you half of what I get. And I'll fund the travel for us to go to the Everglades and rent an airboat and a guide, all that stuff."

It sounded a lot more complicated than Reg had imagined.

"The Everglades is just a little way away from here, right? I think I was in part of it when I went out to see Letticia before Corvin's hearing?" They wouldn't need to book a bus or plane to get there. Reg had just driven in her car.

"Yes, you can get to the edge of it from here. But it's a very big area—a million and a half acres. And a lot of it you can't get to by car. You need a boat."

"Oh." Reg nodded. She watched Starlight, who eventually came over to sit at her feet. He gazed up at her. "Hey, Star." Reg didn't criticize him for taking so long to get ready. She knew better than anyone else how hard he could be to deal with if he were grumpy or someone insulted him. "I'm going to gaze into the crystal and it might work better if I had your help. I'm trying to find a lost wizard."

Damon watched with some amusement. He shouldn't have thought that there was anything funny about it. He had seen Starlight in action before. He had seen what Reg could do. It wasn't like it was an act just for his entertainment.

Except that it kind of was.

Reg patted her lap and Starlight jumped up. He turned around a few times, looking for a comfortable position, and then started kneading her with his paws, his claws pricking her through her dress. She petted him and pushed him gently down. "Okay, enough. Just relax now."

He settled in. Reg rubbed her leg where he had needled it.

"Now, we'll start."

CHAPTER TWO

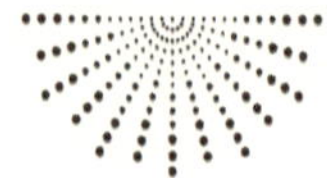

Reg leaned in closer to her crystal ball, petting Starlight and feeling the strengthening and stabilization of her powers. She stared at the outside of the crystal to start with. The shining surface reflected back her own face. After a few minutes, she was able to look past the surface of the crystal into its dark depths.

Wizard Jeffrey Wilson.

She thought his name. It was strange that it should be such a commonplace sounding name. Almost as if he had picked it to be anonymous. But he was a wizard. Not just a mediocre wizard, but according to what Damon had said, he was pretty powerful. There couldn't be that many really powerful wizards named Jeffrey Wilson. She let her eyes defocus and waited, feeling Starlight's warmth on her lap and his comfortable aura enveloping her. Damon shifted restlessly. Reg tried to tune him out.

Where is Wizard Jeffrey Wilson?

Is he in the Everglades?

She remembered the trip to Letticia's house. The area she had traveled through had been very wild. Untamed. Everything was lush green. But she hadn't been to the swampy areas that one could only reach by boat. She had just driven to Letticia's. On increasingly ungroomed roads, but there had been roads of a sort all the way there.

She imagined herself going farther into the Everglades. Where there were no roads, but only boats. She had seen episodes on TV of some of her favorite crime shows that had investigators skimming over the surface of the water and long grass to find a body or some other clue that had been nearly swallowed up by the swamp. Was that what it was like? She couldn't imagine anyone staying lost in those kinds of conditions for very long.

She didn't imagine them *surviving* for very long, anyway.

A picture started to form in her head. She could see a shape pushing its way through long grasses and weirdly-shaped trees dripping with green moss. It was a tall, cloaked man. Reg focused on the vision, trying to sharpen the details. She could see his face under the folds of the hood. A craggy, lined face. Frightened. Looking for a way out.

Maybe he should have just stayed in one place rather than continuing to wander through the emerald jungle. Stayed still so that someone could find him. But he kept going, trying to get out. How could an old man like that be expected to walk out of a one-and-a-half million acre maze?

How had he gotten there? She hadn't thought to ask Damon when he was telling her the few details that he knew. Did Wilson drive in? Take a boat? Was he on his own when he disappeared or was he with a tour group? Had he crashed there in a plane? Was he searching for some rare plant or animal? Sight-seeing?

She felt moved to help him. It was a very strong pull. Reg's instincts were usually for herself over anyone else, so the feeling that she needed to help him was surprising. Without regard for her own needs or how much the payout Damon had been talking about was, she wanted to drop everything and rescue the wizard.

* * *

Skunk Man Swamp, Book #10 of the *Reg Rawlins, Psychic Investigator* series by P.D. Workman can be purchased at pdworkman.com

* * *

ABOUT THE AUTHOR

P.D. Workman is a USA Today Bestselling author and multi-award winner, renowned for her prolific output of over 100 published works that span various genres. With a knack for crafting page-turners, Workman captivates readers with everything from cozy mysteries like the Auntie Clem's Bakery series to gripping young adult and suspense novels.

A prolific reader and writer since childhood, P.D. Workman crafts emotionally powerful stories that don't shy away from hard topics. Her books tackle mental illness, addiction, abuse, and trauma with raw honesty and compassion, giving voice to the often unheard. If you crave authentic, character-driven page-turners that hit deep and stay with you long after the final page, you're in the right place.

With each new release, fans eagerly anticipate another thrilling blend of thought-provoking storytelling and relatable characters that define P.D. Workman's brand as an author of unforgettable page-turners—gripping tales that leave a lasting impact long after the last page is turned.

P. D. Workman, does not shy from probing the deep psychological scars of childhood trauma, mental illness, and addiction. Also characteristic of this author, these extremely sensitive issues are explored with extensive empathy, described with incredible clarity, and portrayed with profound insight.

——KIM, GOODREADS REVIEWER

Some of Workman's titles have been translated into Spanish, French, Portuguese, German, and Italian.

Workman began writing at an early age and is a prolific reader as well as writer. She is also passionate about teaching and learning, expresses her creativity through art and cooking, and loves exploring the Calgary parks and green spaces where the Parks Pat Mysteries are set. She was a legal assistant for many years and has done extensive charitable work.

Workman was born and raised in Alberta, Canada, and is married with one adult son.

* * *

Please visit P.D. Workman at pdworkman.com to see what else she is working on, to join her mailing list, and to link to her social networks.

* * *

If you enjoyed this book, please take the time to recommend it to other purchasers with a review or star rating and share it with your friends!

tiktok.com/@pdworkmanauthor

facebook.com/pdworkmanauthor

x.com/pdworkmanauthor

instagram.com/pdworkmanauthor

amazon.com/author/pdworkman

bookbub.com/authors/p-d-workman

goodreads.com/pdworkman

linkedin.com/in/pdworkman

pinterest.com/pdworkmanauthor

youtube.com/pdworkman

Find P.D. Workman's books at

PDWORKMAN.COM

Scan the QR code below

9 781989 415863